CHASING ROMEO

SARAH READY

CROWN

W.W. CROWN BOOKS
An imprint of Swift & Lewis Publishing LLC
www.wwcrown.com

Library of Congress Control Number: 2020952893
ISBN: 978-1-954007-07-9 (eBook)
ISBN: 978-1-954007-08-6 (pbk)
ISBN: 978-1-954007-09-3 (hbk)
ISBN: 978-1-954007-20-8 (large print)

ALSO BY SARAH READY

The Fall in Love Checklist

Hero Ever After

Find more books by Sarah Ready at:

www.sarahready.com/romance-books

Sign up to receive bonus content, exclusive epilogues and more at:
www.sarahready.com/newsletter

SHE FINALLY FOUND HER SOULMATE.
ALL 7 OF THEM.

A laugh out loud, soulmate chasing rom-com romp. Sarah Ready's *Chasing Romeo* is a perfect feel-good novel about finding love where you least expect it.

Chloe Daniels is a starry-eyed romantic who believes in true love, soulmates and happily ever afters. So when a psychic predicts the identity of her soulmate Chloe will do anything to find him.

But there's a *tiny* problem.

Chloe's soulmate is 1 of 7 men, spread across the U.S. and she has only one week to reach him.

Out of desperation she hires Nick O'Shea, a cynical private investigator who thinks soulmates, love and happily ever afters are a load of crap.

Chloe and Nick have nothing in common. She wants her soulmate. He wants to get paid.

But on their crazy, true love chasing road trip across the U.S. Nick starts to wonder if maybe he was wrong about love, and Chloe starts to wonder if she was wrong about the identity of her Romeo.

Soon, Chloe will have to choose between her soulmate and the man she hired to find him.

Opposites attract in the first book of a heartwarming new series by romance author Sarah Ready.

1

Chloe

EVERY WOMAN ALIVE IS GIVEN ONE MAN WHO IS GUARANTEED TO turn her life into a monument of suck. My one man is Nick O'Shea. Every time he shows up my life gets shaken upside down and spanked.

"Untie me now, Sparky, or so help me God," Nick says.

I smile and ignore his god-awful nickname for me. This is the absolute best day of my life. I stand over him and soak in the feeling that all wrongs in the world are about to be righted.

"Why?" I ask.

"Un. Tie. Me." He strains against the zip ties on his wrists. I'm not going to lie, I get a flash of pleasure deep inside at his struggle.

"Did you want some birthday cake? It's chocolate, your favorite." I wave a pink paper plate with a big slab of cake under his nose.

Nick growls at me. Growls.

My body reacts just like it did when I was fifteen and hopped up on hormones. Unconsciously I lean toward him. Enough of that. I pick up the plastic fork and shove a piece of cake in my mouth. The fudgy frosting's thick, rich and, let's be honest, delicious. "Mmmm. Good."

"Sparky..." he says. His voice is low and full of warning.

"No. Nope. Not gonna," I say.

He looks different than he did in high school. Ten years in the military made him harder. At eighteen, his jaw was softer, his cheeks fuller...his eyes had more warmth. Now, not so much. There's a half-inch-long scar over his right eyebrow that wasn't there before. His cheeks are sharper. His hair's darker and he has stubble on his jaw. I've never seen him with a five o'clock shadow. I think about what it would feel like if I ran my fingers over it.

I glance into his eyes. They're blacker than I remember. He's looking at me like he wants to throttle me. Oh well. I move my gaze to his shoulders. They're thick and muscular and he's wearing a white T-shirt that stretches over him.

Unfortunately, karma didn't catch up to Nick and make his outside match the cynical jerk within. Nope. If I were to draw what he *really* looks like there'd be horns, a forked tongue, and a tail.

I take another bite of cake. He watches and his furious eyes linger on my lips then move down my throat. I can feel the heat of his gaze like he's stroking my neck. Then, his gaze slowly moves over my chest and down my body. I'm in a floral wrap dress with a low neckline. His eyes linger on my breasts, which are smashed up by my push-up bra and prominently displayed.

I have the urge to cover them. Instead, I hold my ground.

"Finished?" I ask.

"Untie me," he says.

I sigh. "Or, how about...gee, Chloe, happy birthday? It's been such a long time. So great to see you," I say.

He scowls. Okay, I admit that was a stretch. I don't think Nick has ever said that it's great to see me...except, well, once.

He turns away and looks over the community room. It's like a birthday fairy exploded and shot out hundreds of pastel balloons, streamers and confetti.

He turns back to me. "Birthdays are a scam," he says. "Just another day for people to fail at meeting unrealistic expectations so they can continue to disappoint each other. Likewise, Christmas and Valentine's Day. Come on, Sparky." He strains at the restraints.

I shake my head. "Hate to disappoint," I say.

"Really?"

"No. Not at all."

Nick sits in an antique wooden chair. His wrists are zip tied to the armrests and his ankles are tied to the spindle legs. What I can't figure out is how he got himself into this situation. The chair's in the middle of a pile of birthday gifts and he has a big red satin bow on his chest. Like he's a gift. *For me.* There's even a gift tag. Although, I've not worked up the courage to get close enough to read it.

I'm not sure why anyone would think that I'd want Nick O'Shea for my birthday. Even if I do live in Romeo, New York: Official Town of Love, USA. People do crazy things here for romance, and usually I'm first in line for the show. Annual Romeo Soul Mate Festival, count me in. Valentine's Day parade, I'm on a float throwing candy hearts. Cookie bake-off for Sweetest Day, yes sir-ee. I'm a diehard romantic. But this...I don't get it.

I've only seen Nick once in the past ten years, and let me tell you, the last time I saw him wasn't a happy occasion. I would've been okay going another decade without his presence. I lick the fudge on my fork. It's really good. Aunt Erma outdid herself this time.

The band on the stage starts to play. My birthday party's picking up. There must be at least seventy or eighty people here. Add the decorations, and a long table full of party food, and it's a hit.

"Happy birthday to our birthday girl, Chloe," the lead singer of the band Rock On Romeo says over the mic. There's clapping and long whistles. I wave and smile.

Now, before you start to think I have loads of friends, let me disillusion you. My party is at my Aunt Erma's retirement home and we invited all the residents in addition to my family and friends. So.

Anyway, we're in the community room at Water's Edge Retirement Center. There are eight big circular tables with chairs, a stage for the band, a parquet dance floor, decorations, and lots of food and cake. I love birthdays, they're my favorite holiday. Anybody's birthday, not just my own. I love to celebrate and I love to show people how much I care by showering them with cards and presents. Nick's a cynic, but I'm not going to let his negativity ruin my day.

I turn to him. "Don't know why you're here, sitting in my present pile," I say, "but I'm not unwrapping until after I blow out my candles."

"Is this payback?" he asks.

I hold back a flinch.

There's a look in his eyes. In anyone else I'd say it's vulnerability, but Nick doesn't do vulnerable. Or regret.

"For what?" I ask. "What could I possibly have to pay you back for? The pigtails? The barbies? The flagpole?" I pause. "My wedding?"

He scowls.

"What? Tongue-tied?" I ask.

He shakes his head and gold flickers in his black eyes. "You're crazy," he says.

"Hey, I'm not the one who tied you up. Besides, it's my birthday. I'm allowed to be crazy."

I give him a long, slow smile. The music from the band and all the conversations are so loud I have to lean closer to hear his response.

"No, Sparky. You're crazy every day." His eyes crinkle at the edges. This close I can see the little lines at their corners and the gold and amber flecks in his irises.

I think he's joking. There's an almost smile on his lips. But then, it's gone, and I'm not sure anymore. I knock away any softening I feel toward him. This is Nick I'm dealing with, not some sweet innocent puppy.

"Still not letting you go. You look good tied up, it's always been a fantasy of mine."

He narrows his eyes. "Really?"

"Absolutely. The Great Nick O'Shea...completely at my mercy."

His fingers clench the armrest and he swallows. There's a crackling tension in the air around him. Then, "When Hell freezes over."

I lean forward, our noses almost touching, and I mock shiver. "Is it cold in here?"

He glares, then his eyes drift down to my lips. His eyelashes dip and suddenly he looks like he wants to lick my mouth. I step back. Then I carefully set my cake down on the table next to him.

"In case you're hungry," I say. "Some devil's food cake for your stay in Hell."

Too bad he's tied up and can't enjoy it.

"Eat your heart out," I say.

Then, I walk away, swaying my hips to the music, enjoying the burn of his eyes on my back.

2

Nick

I SHOULD'VE KNOWN COMING BACK TO ROMEO, NEW YORK, WAS A bad idea. The town's obsessed with love—puppy love, love at first sight, second-chance love, true love, any old type of love. They go nuts for it. Ten years away, I'd forgotten the extent of the delusion.

I'm not sure how I forgot. I grew up here, even drank the Kool-Aid in my idiotic teenage years. The town's always listed in those nonsense guides as the most romantic place in America. I mean, they're not wrong. Even I can admit the old brick buildings on Main Street, painted in bright colors, with flowering baskets hanging on every available surface are... charming. Plus, the bronze statue of Juliet leaning down her balcony reaching out to Romeo, yes, it has its draws. And okay, the SweetStop Bakery is fantastic. And the toyshop, and the bookshop, and yes, the Victorian rose garden at the center of town is nice in the summer. Unbelievable...three weeks in town and they're already converting me back to romance fandom. I close my eyes and flex against the zip ties.

Sure, I could bust out. But then, I'd ruin Erma's fun. Unfortunately, she fed me too many oatmeal raisin cookies as a kid for me to end her scheming. I'm both embarrassed and impressed that she conned me with a fake walker routine and knocked my butt into this chair. Currently, she's dancing with a teenager. No walker in sight. It's a lively birthday party. Most of the people are doing a good job of ignoring the big guy tied up in the present pile. They probably think it's somehow *romantic.*

After all, the town's official *Soul Mate Psychic* is in charge. And it's her favorite grand-niece's birthday bash. Nobody is going to naysay Erma.

I narrow my eyes and watch Chloe dance with one of the retirement home residents. She tosses her head back and laughs. The sound is throaty and seductive and horribly familiar. A long time ago, I would've given anything to be the one dancing with her, the one making her laugh. Then for a minute, I was. I was like a kid that finally meets Santa face to face and realizes *he's real.* Except, he isn't. Which all grown-ups know. Santa Claus isn't real, and neither is love. Chloe taught me that.

In Romeo though, everyone loves her. In fact, the only thing I've heard about since coming home is Chloe Daniels. It's like she's the official mascot of the town. Everyone has something to say about her. Whether I'm getting a coffee at the bakery, or I'm in the check-out line at the grocery, it's all about Chloe.

Did you know Chloe has her own greeting card line? No, I didn't.

Did you know she hand-delivers cards to the housebound, the sick, the lonely? No, not a clue.

Did you know she's a saint? Nope.

Did you know she's a single saint? No. Didn't know. But it sounds uncomfortable.

I glare as Chloe spins in time to the music and her dress flows around her.

Not interested.

At all.

Not at all.

What? Don't believe me?

Trust me.

The last thing I need is a first love swinging back around and sucker punching me in the head. Unrequited love is a hell of thing. I had it for years. It was like a virus, I caught it, I suffered and now I'm immune. To love, to Chloe, to the whole darn thing.

I have two things I'm concentrating on right now. One, getting my private investigator's business up and running. Two, getting my cabin in the woods so I can be left alone.

When I left the military I could've gone anywhere. But for some reason, all I could picture was a quaint little town in upstate New York, and my own cabin on the mountain.

I want my business and I want my cabin, Chloe doesn't enter into either of those goals.

Miss Erma catches my attention as she saunters over. Barely five foot tall and white haired, she's in a red silk kimono that flows around her like rippling water as she walks. Erma has huge hawk eyes with an arresting stare. Her dad was from Ireland and her mom from Japan, they moved to New York from Hawaii after World War II. She's a small woman with a presence of someone three times her size. Long after you forget everything else about her, you remember her piercing eyes. When I was a kid I confessed all sorts of things to her because of that stare.

Romeo town legend claims she can *see* your soul mate.

Luckily, I'm too much of a skeptic to believe that. But Chloe's not. And neither is the rest of Romeo. Miss Erma has a book three inches thick of all the couples she's matched over the past seventy-five years. In fact, I see at least a dozen couples at this party that were matched by her.

A slither of foreboding crawls down my spine.

"Erma, please tell me I'm not Chloe's soul mate," I say.

She laughs and her shrewd gaze takes me in. My mouth goes dry.

I look around the room, desperate to see Chloe's face. To determine if she *knew* about this when she came over to taunt me. I don't see her in the crowd. I turn back to Erma and her lips curve into a knowing smile.

"You're not Chloe's soul mate," she says.

I let out a long sigh. "Good. Good." I close my eyes and realign myself to the news. Erma doesn't think I'm Chloe's soul mate, ergo Chloe doesn't think I'm her soul mate, ergo...I flounder, not sure what I'm feeling.

"Having a nice time? Did you try the cake?" She glances at the half-eaten cake on the table next to me.

I look at Erma. "Nah. I'm a little tied up," I say.

She laughs and pats my shoulder. "You're a good sport."

"Does that mean you're going to untie me now?"

"Not at all."

I sigh. Miss Erma called me a few hours ago and asked me to visit. I swung by with flowers. Like I said, she used to feed me cookies. After a few minutes of small talk, she got to the point. She had a job that she wanted me to do. I refused. Then...I got tied up.

"Have you reconsidered your rejection of my job offer?"

"No." If I could cross my arms, I would.

"But you didn't let me finish my proposal. I merely said you would be working closely with my grand-niece."

"Where'd you get the zip ties?" I ask.

She smiles. Can you believe it? An eighty-something-year-old smiling over the fact that she knocked me down with a walker and tied me to a chair.

"If you take this job, I promise you will never have to deal with Chloe again. Not unless you want to."

I shake my head. Not good enough. I could do that on my own. I could leave town tomorrow and never see her again. Granted, right at this moment, leaving town holds some appeal.

"I will pay two thousand dollars, plus expenses," she says.

I raise my eyebrows. "That's quite a birthday gift. Still...no."

I'm starting to feel bad refusing, but I don't need the money enough for the pain of *working closely* with Chloe.

Erma touches her finger to her nose, then, "I'll sweeten the deal. If you accept this job, I'll make sure you get what you've always wanted."

What I've always wanted?

I glance across the community room at the birthday party. It's in full swing. Everyone is laughing, talking, and enjoying themselves. I finally catch sight of Chloe. She's like a beacon. People gravitate toward her because they want to be caught up in her warmth. I can feel her heat from here.

I look back to Erma, unsettled by the knowledge in her sharp eyes.

"I just want to be left alone," I say.

She tilts her head. "What you want most."

I swallow the lump in my throat. "Why?"

Her hawk eyes turn up as she smiles. She pulls a polaroid picture out of her kimono. Slowly she turns it around and holds it in front of my face.

A sharp exhale leaves my lungs.

I lean forward and the zip ties cut into my skin. The pain in my wrists doesn't matter. I need to get closer to the image.

I stare at the photo and my heart taps out a hard beat.

It's...

I let out a long, slow exhale.

What I've always wanted?

This feels like a devil's bargain. What does Erma know that I don't? And why is she willing to give me all of this for a job? I take the advice of a tired cliché. Don't look a gift horse in the mouth. One little job with *her*—Chloe—and I'll have what I've always wanted. Really, there's no debate.

Finally, I tear my eyes away from the picture and up to Erma's shrewd gaze.

"Okay," I say, "I'll take the job."

3

Chloe

I TAP MY FOOT TO THE UPBEAT FIFTIES POP AND SMILE LIKE IT'S MY job. For the past fifteen minutes I've been handing out cards to all my guests. When I was little, I thought that my birthday meant I had to give everybody else cards and gifts. I spent the whole week leading up to my fourth birthday making cards and presents. My parents thought it was so hilarious that we made it a family tradition. Little did they know my birthday card frenzy was just a lead-up to my career as a card illustrator and designer.

I'm at one of the round tables telling everybody about our new birthday puns line. The favorite so far is the one with an eighty-year-old pirate who's saying "Aye matey!" Mrs. Lee in particular couldn't stop laughing.

I pause when I see my best friend Veronica walk up. "I wasn't going to give you your present until later, but this is an emergency. Excuse us, please," she says. Then she pulls me away from the table where a group of residents are eating cake and drinking punch.

"Hey. I was handing out cards," I say. I have a stack of at least fifty left in my hands. I always make sure to get cards to all the retirement home residents on my birthday. There's two centers and about two hundred people. "Isn't this a great party? Aunt Erma outdid herself. Also, everyone loves our birthday puns line, Mrs. Lee especially loves..."

Veronica holds up her hand in a *stop now* gesture. "Chloe. As your best friend, business partner, and confidant since age three, I'm going to call your B.S." She holds up a rectangular present wrapped in silver paper with a pink ribbon. "Open it."

Okaaay, so apparently she wasn't fooled by my faked nonchalance.

"You noticed him too, huh?"

She snorts. "Who? You mean the big brooding sex god in the present pile? No, didn't notice him at all."

I take a quick peek in Nick's direction. He's in a heated conversation with Aunt Erma. I wouldn't go up against her, she gets her way, one hundred percent of the time. It's easier to admit defeat immediately and then go with the flow. Otherwise, it's a rough ride and you end up doing what she wanted anyway. Just ask the nineteen hundred gazillion couples that she's matched.

Wait. A. Second.

Dread blooms in my stomach and the cake I've been eating in mass quantity settles like a brick. "I don't feel so good," I say. I put a hand to my stomach.

"Figured it out, did ya?" asks Veronica. She rests a hand on my arm and squeezes.

I shake my head and try to push off the sudden urge to bolt.

"This can't...I can't. No. No, no, no." I'm babbling. Eight months ago, I would've loved for Aunt Erma to prognosticate my soul mate. I could've avoided a very unpleasant *left at the altar* situation. But now?

I point at Nick. "Why's he here?" I say.

Veronica tsks. "Poor Chloe. All that birthday cake has fried your brain. She's gifting you your soul mate."

"Ack," I say.

Veronica winces with sympathy. "I mean, maybe it's not Nick O'Shea, maybe he's just tied up for entertainment? Pin the heart on the cynic? Bobbing for poisoned apples...or he's the piñata? Hit him with a stick and sardonic candy falls out."

I cover my face with my hands. "How could I be so stupid?"

"Your aunt's wily. I live in terror of her."

I shrug. "I live in terror of doctors and puppets."

Veronica laughs. "Oh my gosh. Pupaphobia, totally forgot about that. Remember your eighth birthday when your parents hired that puppet show?"

"Peed my pants I was so afraid."

She snickers and I punch her on the arm.

Then, all joking aside, I lean into her. "Oh, Vee. What am I going to do?"

Veronica puts on her business leader face that means she has a solution. "First, open my present. I gotcha covered. Second, hit number one independent greeting card company in the USA for the second year running. Third...um, there's no third. Sorry."

"Alright then." I pull the pink ribbon and slowly unwrap Veronica's present. "It's...?"

She laughs. "It's a survival kit. Wet fire, water purification tablets, cordage, a multitool, it's got all the goods."

I stare down at the bizarre assortment of tools that I might need in an apocalypse kind of situation. Veronica's such a prepper. She's been on me for years to get a survival kit and start stockpiling canned goods. She fantasizes about doomsday like I fantasize about boy meets girl, boy and girl fall in love, boy and girl stay together forever.

"Are these pliers? Rope? Is this duct tape?"

"You gotta show 'em who's boss, right away," she says.

I hold up the multitool. It has knife blades, wire cutters, a file and more all tucked together. "Ummm..."

She winks. "You'll figure it out."

I laugh. I can only imagine what she means by that. "Thanks, you weirdo."

She flips her ponytail and smirks. Veronica looks like the stereotypical blonde cheerleader, but she's a genius internet marketer, business maven, and weekend hiker/survivalist.

"I'm glad you're my best friend," I say.

She nods then glances at Nick. "If you don't want him, I'll take care of it. I found this really secluded cave in the backwoods last weekend." She wrinkles her nose. "Only the bears will find him."

I shake my head. "He's not that bad."

She raises her eyebrows. The trouble with best friends is that they know everything about you, so they know when you're lying.

I glance over my shoulder. Looks like Aunt Erma untied Nick. He's currently at the edge of the dance floor holding his hand out to Miss Myrtle. She lost her husband last year and hasn't been the same since. I watch as Myrtle smiles up at him like he's a knight in shining armor. He guides her onto the dance floor and spins her in a circle. He leans down to say something and Myrtle laughs. She *laughs*. My heart melts a bit. I haven't seen her laugh in ages and within thirty seconds Nick gave her that gift.

Veronica crosses her arms over her chest and shakes her head. She's not buying the Sir Galahad routine.

"Do you remember when Nick showed up on the day of your wedding as the substitute best man?" asks Veronica.

"Yes?"

"You said to me, Vee, I guarantee this day isn't going to end well."

And I was right. At the altar my groom grabbed my bridesmaid's hand and ran out of the church.

"What did Nick say after Ron left with Candy?" Veronica asks.

"He said"—I put on my deep growly Nick voice—"what are you all crying about, isn't there still cake to eat?"

Veronica snorts.

I start to laugh, I can't help it. It wells up in me and bursts out. He deserved my taunting with the devil's food cake—he totally deserved it. His statement wasn't funny eight months ago, but remembering him at the altar with that deadpan straight face going on about not wasting a good cake...jeez.

Veronica sighs and tosses her blonde ponytail behind her shoulder. "I'm going to say one thing and one thing only. Just because everyone thinks your aunt can see soul mates doesn't mean she can. You're in charge of your own life."

"I know. Hence, Ron," I say. Who turned out to be a big fat cheating failure. And hence Nick, who turned out to be my big fat broken-hearted failure.

Veronica nods. "You're an incurable romantic, which isn't a bad thing in our line of work, but I gotta say, maybe you need to get out of the fantasy of love so you can find the real thing."

I frown. "I'm not in a fantasy." I mean, sure I grew up on stories of love and soul mates. Look at the town I live in, and look at who my great-aunt is. My bedtime stories were tales of Aunt Erma's love matches. It's not a fantasy, it's reality. I see it every day. Aunt Erma always told me, someday, I'd find my soul mate too. It's not a fantasy when you have hundreds of couples that went before you to prove the truth.

Aunt Erma's gift doesn't work on demand though. But she'd told me I'd find him, so I tried...and tried...and tried.

I study Nick as he leads Myrtle back to her seat. Ninety-year-old Mrs. Woods flags him down and ushers him back out to the dance floor. He doesn't seem to mind. In fact, he looks... happy. There are dozens of couples dancing to the nineteen fifties pop hits. I'd like to be dancing.

"Happy birthday, Chloe," says Mr. Garcia. He pushes his walker closer.

"Oh thank you, here, have a card. It's from our pun line." I hand him the card, illustrated with my signature ink and vibrant watercolor.

Veronica waits until he leaves, then, "Before you go handing out more cards, do you believe in soul mates?"

"Of course," I say. What kind of stupid question is that?

Veronica nods. "Exactly. Most people don't. Maybe you should get out of that fantasy and find real love on your own."

I shake my head. "What? No. Tried it. Got the T-shirt. It sucked. If Aunt Erma tells me my soul mate then I'm all in, one hundred percent." I ignore the rolling in my stomach.

"Even if it's Nick O'Shea?"

I nibble on a fingernail. "Did you try the cake?" I ask.

She snorts. "There's duct tape in the kit. And the cave offer's still open."

"Thanks for the gift, you're a pal," I say. "Anyway, you know Aunt Erma's never wrong." Which before, I loved. But now...

"Yeah. I live in terror," she says.

Then I circulate the room, handing out cards and thanking everyone for coming. Except Nick. I avoid him.

Finally, when my cards are gone, and I've danced a few times with some of the residents—Mr. Garcia's a natural—I sit down next to Veronica at a circular table. Four of the residents are playing gin rummy. It's a fierce competition. But, I learned young, never join a card game at a retirement home unless you can take the heat.

"This party was a hit," I say to Veronica. "Best birthday yet."

I sip the fizzy punch. Aunt Erma wished me happy birthday and didn't mention Nick's presence. My parents already left. They're going on their thirty-year anniversary cruise tomorrow morning and have to get to NYC tonight. They gave me a generous gift card to the local art store, Art Haven, which I completely approve of. They know me so well. I'm going to be stocking up on new paper, pencils, ink, and watercolors.

"Looks like you dodged a bullet," says Veronica.

I nod. I guess Nick was just a gag gift from Aunt Erma.

The music stops. I look up at the stage as Aunt Erma taps the microphone. The talking in the room fades until the only noise is the hissing of a streamer caught in a ceiling fan.

"Thank you all for coming," says Aunt Erma. "To celebrate our Chloe's birthday."

The remaining eighty or so people clap and whistle. I stand up and give a quick curtsy.

Aunt Erma continues. "As you all know, eight months ago, Chloe had a fortunate escape on her wedding day."

I close my eyes and shake my head. There's clapping and a few boos in the room. In a town of only a few thousand people, *everyone* knows your business. In fact, nearly everyone in this room was *at* the wedding.

"She can do better," says Mr. Garcia over the clapping.

"Marry me, Chloe," someone shouts. I'm not sure who, but it gets a laugh from everyone.

Aunt Erma clears her throat. "Today, I have a very special birthday present for my very special niece."

My body tingles. Aunt Erma smiles at me. Then winks.

"As you all know, my gift doesn't manifest on demand. I would have liked very much to save my niece years of heartache."

"Hear, hear!" Mrs. Lee shouts.

"But now I can give her a very special gift..." says Erma. "Her soul mate."

The words ring over the community room and the microphone screeches. There's silence. Then, everyone starts to clap and cheer and pound their fists on the tables.

"Oh no," says Veronica.

I stand. I can't help myself. Finally, the room falls quiet again and everyone either looks at me or Aunt Erma. This is the stuff of Romeo legend. It's not every day Erma announces a love match, but when she does, she's never wrong.

Suddenly, it feels like déjà vu. I've seen this moment in a dream, except, I'm the one standing on the stage, and when I look down, I'm completely naked and everyone stares, waiting for me to announce my true love's name.

I blink and the room comes back into focus. I'm not naked. I'm in my birthday dress. I take a step forward. My heart thunders in my ears. I take another step.

My soul mate.

This is the moment I've been dreaming of since I was a little girl.

Then, a movement near the stage catches my attention. It's Nick. He's watching me, a peculiar look on his face. I stop walking and stare into his eyes. What would it be like to hold him again? To touch him?

His eyes are hooded and there's a small smile playing at the corner of his mouth. My heart lurches.

"So, after twenty-eight years of waiting, Chloe's soul mate is..."

Aunt Erma pauses.

I smile at Nick. A hesitant, cautious unfurling of my lips. Is it him?

Then, Nick narrows his eyes and sneers. At me. He sneers at me.

Oh.

He turns away.

Oh.

I push a hand against my stomach. I think I'm going to be sick. He hates me. And I hate him.

Don't be Nick. Don't be Nick. Please, if there's a God in this world, don't be Nick.

"Don't be Nick," I whisper.

He turns back to me. His eyes sharp, like he heard my plea. But that's impossible. We're fifty feet apart. He stares and I'm sucked into his gaze.

"...her soul mate is..." says Erma.

My eyes are locked on Nick's. I can tell we're both remembering. His mouth over mine, the long, luxurious kisses that lasted hours at a time. The summer sun pouring over us as we cradled each other in the grass. His hands, running down my neck, across my ribs, over my breasts. His mouth. His kisses. Hot, wet kisses.

"The boy she first kissed," says Aunt Erma.

The space between Nick and me crackles. The room erupts into exclamations.

"Oh, thank god," says Veronica.

"Who is it?" someone asks.

"Who's the lucky man?" another shouts.

I tear my eyes from Nick's.

The first boy I ever kissed?

"Remember? Third grade summer camp," says Veronica. She's come up next to me, I presume for moral support. She grabs my hand and squeezes.

Aunt Erma smiles at me from the stage. Behind her the band starts to play the 1960s hit, *It's in His Kiss.*

If you want to know if he loves you so...it's in his kiss.

"Was that him? Summer camp?" asks Veronica.

I nod. I was nine years old, and I kissed him behind the art shed on the last day of camp. Apparently, he was my soul mate, I just didn't know it yet.

I look back at Nick. He's still watching me, a scowl on his face. His eyes are hooded and unreadable. Fine.

I turn away from him and address the room.

"Matt Smith," I say in a clear, carrying voice. "Matt Smith is my soul mate." It's strange, because for a small moment, I'm disappointed. Then, I shove it aside.

Everyone cheers. Well, everyone except Nick.

So, I smile. A big, beatific, birthday girl smile. *Holy crap*, I think, but my smile says, *yaaaay*.

"Wow," says Veronica. "You haven't seen him since he was nine. What if he's..." She stops.

"He'll be perfect," I say. "I'll love him, and he'll love me." This is something I know to be true, it's the immutable law of soul matehood. In the past, no man has loved me for me, they've always left, but a soul mate, no matter your quirks, they stay. They love you. They don't hurt you and they don't leave.

Erma clears her throat and the room goes silent again. Suddenly, there's an itch at the base of my spine. What now?

"The second part of my gift," says Aunt Erma "is that Nick O'Shea, Romeo's very first private investigator, is going to help Chloe find her soul mate."

I whip my head around to look at Nick. His arms are folded across his chest and he has a smirk on his face.

Aunt Erma continues, "Because, as it happens, our Chloe has only one week to find her soul mate. If she doesn't find him by then...he'll be gone forever."

4

Chloe

THE AUTUMN AFTERNOON TURNS BLUSTERY, AND CRIMSON AND yellow leaves blow off the trees. They swirl in mini whirls across the sky. At my desk, I sketch the turmoil of the falling leaves and the dark gray storm clouds.

I'm in my downtown art studio/one-bedroom apartment over the bakery. Everyone at the party congratulated me and was gung ho about me finding my Matt Smith. Well, except Nick. He told me to meet him in Amos, the next town over, for dinner at eight. I looked for Matt Smith online, but couldn't find anything promising. I guess that's why Aunt Erma hired a private investigator.

The real question, the one that has me going through sheet after sheet of paper is...do I do this? I said I would. I believed, since I was little, that I would. I always thought that given the chance, I would pursue my fated one to the ends of the earth.

And now, here I am, with the opportunity of a lifetime and

I'm hesitating. Why does Nick have to be a part of this? I asked Aunt Erma if I could find my soul mate without him, and she said no. So, I have two options. I can forget about the whole thing, lose my soul mate and keep making awful choices when it comes to love. Or I can lock away whatever it was that I once felt for Nick, and pursue my soul mate with unwavering singlemindedness.

I sigh and set down my pen.

The rain beats against the window, and the thrumming of the downpour takes me back to eight months ago—the last time I saw Nick.

I crouch in my wedding dress on the stone steps of the church. The rain falls, pouring down my face. Thunder booms and I wrap my arms around myself. I stare out over downtown Romeo.

"Chloe. You're soaking wet. Come inside," Veronica says. I tilt my face up to the downpour.

"I love the rain," I say. I smile up at her and blink through the downpour. "No one can see your tears in the rain, Vee."

"Come on, hon," she says. "He was a toad. I never told you this, but I always hated him. Hated him since third grade."

I shake my head. "I thought I found him. My soul mate, Vee. But I didn't. And now he's gone." I ask the question I'm scared of. "Is it me?"

I run my hand over the dirty gray of my soaking wet wedding dress.

"No," says Veronica. "Never. It's Ron. And your crappy excuse for a second cousin, Candy. Ugh, if I ever see her again, it's on..."

I smile and take Vee's hand. I appreciate her angry vehemence, because right now, all I feel is pain.

I hear Mrs. Wilkes in the entry of the church, "Chloe's always been terrible at choosing men. She's a sweetie, but her taste in men is bottom barrel terrible. She couldn't pick a good one if her life depended on it."

"Tell me about it. The groom running out with a bridesmaid. The poor hopeless dear," says another voice.

"She always wants each man to be *the one* so badly that she can't see how wrong for her they are."

"Remember that porn addict Travis? How long did she date him?" asks someone else.

"And Ryan. He fleeced her for two thousand dollars and stole her microwave."

"And don't get me started on that O'Shea boy," says Mrs. Wilkes. "The flagpole fiasco."

"Wasn't he the best man?"

I block them out and tilt my face back up to the rain. As long as it keeps pouring, no one will see how much this hurts.

Veronica squeezes my hand and sits down next to me. "Don't listen," she says.

I thought I'd found the one. I believed I could count on him to love me for life. We didn't even make it past dearly beloved.

I look up at the sky. "They're right," I say.

I watch a flash of lightning strike. I'm not melodramatic, really I'm not, but that crack of lightning felt like my breaking heart.

"I wish this would all go away. That I could disappear."

"No, hon," she says.

"God as my witness, Vee, I'm never going to trust myself with love ever again. I won't be with a man again. Not until I'm certain he's my soul mate. Only then."

Another boom of thunder hits.

The windowpane rattles in front of me and I'm pulled back to the present.

I look down at the sheet of paper on my desk. It'd been a landscape. I hadn't realized I was crying again, but my tears had splashed onto the ink and now the illustration was a mess of black.

In movies and books, the characters always get over heartbreak so easily. Like their fiancé or spouse having an affair wasn't the most awful, painful, devastating thing that ever happened to them. Let me tell you. It was. In real life, it was. The worst part was that for months after I hated myself. My trust of people, my positivity, my career, everything that made me me, I hated. Because none of me was good enough. Do you see?

In the movies, the heroines move on and find a new guy in a matter of pages. In three paragraphs they've chucked the pain and moved on. Life isn't really that way. Eight months later, I still don't trust myself enough to know whether a man truly loves me or not. I've been wrong so many times before. Here's my dirty, awful, buried deep down secret—I'll never trust myself again. Being wrong hurts too much.

So.

There's my answer.

I'm going to pursue my soul mate with everything I have and I'm not going to stop until I find him. Even if it means being up close and personal with Nick O'Shea for the next week. Because when it's over, Nick will be out of my life, and I'll have the man who will love me, and I'll love him.

5

Nick

"THERE ARE HOW MANY THOUSANDS?" ASKS CHLOE.

I think she's in shock. "Nine thousand, six hundred and thirteen in the US, but that's for all ages, we narrowed it down to 364 for his age group." She winces. "You see, Matthew was the most common name for boys the year he was born. Smith is the most common surname in the U.S. Put it together and you're looking for a needle in a haystack. Assuming he's still in the country. Or alive."

Chloe looks up at the ceiling of the restaurant and shakes her head. "We're talking about my soul mate. I have one week. Call your contacts, do..."—she waves her hands in the air —"something investigatey."

I try hard not to smile. "Investigatey?"

"Why are we here?" she asks.

I glance around the dimly lit medieval dinner theatre. We're at a wooden table overlooking the arena, where two knights are currently jousting. The green knight lands a solid hit on the red knight. A group sitting a few tables away cheers. The "serving wench" just dropped off trenchers, which are dry flat breads that serve as the plate, green mush, roast quail, and two goblets of honey mead. There are colorful banners on the walls, candles, and roaming minstrels.

"Well?" she asks.

"I like the food," I say. I tear a bit of dry bread off and dip it in the green glop. A minstrel ventures close and I wave him away.

She gives me a skeptical look. "You know, the concept of romantic love was born in medieval times. Before the period of chivalry, marriage was for practical reasons. The knights were fighting for an ideal. I never figured you'd buy into that," she says. She takes a swallow of her mead. I watch as she licks the honey liquid from her lips.

She glares when she notices where my focus lies. I look away, shamed like a kid caught with his hand in the cookie jar.

My attention is caught by my target and his affair partner. Yes, I'm here on a job. They're sitting at a nearby table. I pull out my cell phone and pretend to check messages while I take a dozen photos. I snap a picture of the guy with his hand on the lady's back. Him touching her hair. Her leaning down to kiss him, lots of tongue. Yeah. Case closed.

"Did you hear me?" asks Chloe.

"What?"

I put down my phone. My final infidelity case is now wrapped up. Affairs are, truth be told, a private investigator's bread and butter. But after I email these photos to my client and write up my report, I'm free to leave town with Chloe.

"Can we find him?" she asks.

I push down a flash of irritation. Yes, I accepted this job, but... "Why do you want to?" I ask.

I wonder, what would she have done if Erma had said my name? I guess we'll never find out.

She sits up straighter in her chair and her cheeks flush with pink. "Because," she says. I get the feeling I'm in for an impassioned argument. Then she wrinkles her forehead and shrugs. "You wouldn't understand."

I feel cheated. "Try me," I say.

She shakes her head. Then she goes back to picking at the gross mush on her bread plate.

"Alright," I say. "See the couple at your four o'clock? The man in the Members Only jacket and the woman in the blue velvet dress?"

She looks, then her gaze softens. "They're in love," she says.

I scoff. "Yeeeah, love. You're naïve, Sparky. That man's wife is at home with their four children. That woman's husband is at home with their two-year-old daughter. There's no love there, only selfishness, delusion and a future of pain."

She flinches and her face drains of color. I feel bad, until she lifts her jaw in a stubborn slant. There's the fighter I remember. "You can't know that," she says.

"Can't I? I bet you anything those two are telling each other that they're 'soul mates.' That only they can understand each other. That they never really had love until now, that they are star-crossed lovers, and that they don't want to do this, but how can they deny their all-encompassing love, et cetera, et cetera. In fact, they'll tell each other anything to justify in their minds the sheer garbage of what they're doing to people who trust them. Betrayal, Sparky, it's love's ugly twin. Disappointment is their big brother."

The minstrel moves over again and starts to sing a medieval love ballad.

"Wow, Nick. Thanks for that, I almost forgot that you were a big fat jerk."

The minstrel misses a note and then discreetly moves away from the table. Chloe rips at her bread and chews more forcefully than necessary.

The couple has started to make out. I could get more photos, but I decide to leave it alone. I turn back to Chloe. I forgot how soft she is. Everything about her is soft. She's like an impressionist painting. Curly hair, heart-shaped face, wide cupid's bow mouth, and her breasts...lush. When you get too close she's all out of focus and dreamy. It makes a man want to grab her and kiss her back into focus. I shake my head and clear the vision. Not for me.

"I'm just asking," I say, "are you sure you want to bet your future on a myth?" Because, to be honest, something inside me wishes she'd get up and say, *screw you, fate, I'm taking my future in my own hands.*

"Would I bet my future?" she asks.

I nod and lean forward to hear her answer.

Slowly, she says, "I'd bet everything."

Her words ring in my ears. She's serious. She'll do anything to get with this random guy she hasn't seen in nearly twenty years. It's like a cosmic joke, except I'm not laughing. I guess I shouldn't have expected anything less.

"It's a myth," I say. "It's not real."

"It is," she says. She points her finger at me and jabs me in the chest. "And I'm going to prove it to you." Her hand rests over my heart. We both look down at her touching me. She yanks it back and wipes her hand on her napkin.

No man likes to see a woman wipe herself off after touching him. I scowl and then take her unspoken challenge. "More likely, by the end of this week, I'll prove that soul mates don't exist."

"Good luck, you have hundreds of Aunt Erma's successes against you."

No worries, I stand by my belief that the whole town of Romeo is suffering from romantic delusions. Hey, the tourism dollars depend on it.

Also, I'd like to push a little bit of reality into this situation and throw out the idea that this guy might not be decent.

"He could be a rapist," I say. That gets her attention. Her head snaps up and she glares at me.

"Or a Lothario," she says. *Take that*, her eyes say. She bares her teeth at me in a semblance of a grin and I smile back. Game on.

The minstrel who had wandered close again hightails it to the other side of the restaurant.

"He could be a drug dealer," I say.

"Or a pharmacist," she says.

"He could be an alcoholic."

"A vintner."

"He's unemployed," I say.

"Independently wealthy."

"He looks like a frog."

"He's a prince," she says.

"He's boring."

"Strong and silent."

I glare at her and she glares back, a smile curving on her lips.

"Bad in bed," I say.

"A sex god." She bites at her lower lip and I have the urge to take it in my mouth and show her a decade of pent-up wanting. I yank my thoughts from her lips and drop my ace in the hole.

"He could be an ax murderer," I say. Take that and chew on it.

She laughs, throaty and low, and her eyes light up. The candlelight sparks off her glowing skin.

"Or," she says, "he's a lumberjack. Mmmm. Sexy ax. I'll hold the handle. Rawr." She claws her hand and scratches at the air.

I shake my head. "You got it." I hold up my goblet of mead for a toast. "To Matt Smith. Chloe's lumberjack soul mate."

She lifts her goblet and clinks it against mine. Some of the mead sloshes over the side and drizzles over my hand. I tilt up the cup and take a long drink to cool the fire roaring in my gut. She's watching me over the rim of her glass.

Finally, I set my goblet down and wipe off my hand.

"Were you always like this?" she asks. She's looking at me like I've offered up a puzzle for her to solve. There's nothing puzzling about me. I'm as straightforward as they come.

"I've narrowed the field down to six," I say.

She shakes her head like the topic change gave her whiplash.

"Six Matt Smiths?"

"Yeah. I have a friend, Reed, he was in intelligence. He did some heavy lifting, pulled some favors. Since we have no school records, no address, no social security number, no parents, no—"

"I met him at summer camp. I was nine," she says. She's in a huff.

"Exactly. Since we only had a name, an approximate age, probably ethnicity and general location, we were able to narrow the search to six potential Matt Smiths."

She leans forward and grasps the edge of the table. "Well? Where are they? Can I call them? Email them? Meet them?" Her eyes glow. She's practically jumping up and down she's so excited.

There's a sword fight happening in the arena, and the raucous table cheers again.

"Settle down, Sparkplug," I say.

She blows out a breath and sits back in her seat.

"We had twenty-seven potentials originally. I already contacted and crossed off the ones I could. For the rest, we only have their addresses. They're the below-the-radar type. No web presence. No social media. No phone. No traceable records..." I pause.

"So....?" she asks.

"So, they could be a little...off," I say.

She narrows her eyes. "Didn't we just do this? He's a sexy lumberjack, remember? So, what else is the problem?"

This is the bit I was worried about bringing up. "So"—I spread my arms and smile—"we're going on a road trip."

"Ack," she says.

"Exactly," I say. "A car, the road, you and me."

She's speechless.

I pull a printout of the US from my coat pocket. I hold it up in front of her. I've highlighted our route and put X's on all the stops. It spans from New York to Nevada and covers more than twenty-five hundred miles.

"Wait. You realize we only have a week? Why don't we fly?" she asks.

"No," I say.

"But we don't have time to drive."

"We'll make it."

"But—"

I fold the map and put it on the table.

"I don't fly."

"But—"

"Ever."

She sighs. "Ever, ever?"

I shake my head. "No."

We'll make it. It'll be tight, but I have the trip planned to the mile and have prepared for contingencies. Everything will go according to plan.

We're silent for a minute. She stares at the couple. There's a lot of PDA happening. I sigh and pull out my phone to take a few more photos. It's what I'm getting paid for after all.

"Why are you taking photos?" Chloe asks.

"I'm on a job," I say as I snap another.

"Wait a minute. You knew they weren't..." She ends the sentence on an outraged squeak.

I shrug. "Sure."

She grabs the map and looks over the route. Then, "So, Connecticut, Illinois, Nebraska, Colorado, and two in Nevada?"

Six potential guys all lined up to sweep Chloe off her feet and out of my life forever.

"I'll pick you up at nine a.m.?" I ask.

"Okay," she says. She hands the map back to me. I take it, fold it, and put it in my pocket.

Even though I've already agreed and I really want what Erma has promised, I need to make sure... "Chloe," I start.

She looks up, and I realize she's surprised because I don't usually use her real name. I clear my throat and start over. "You sure about this? There's no guarantee any of these guys are the one. You could get hurt..."

I stop when I see the way she's looking at me. It's real similar to the look she sent my way on her wedding day right after the groom grabbed the bridesmaid and ran down the aisle. I scowl and reboot again.

"It's not real," I say. "It's not worth getting hurt over. Love is just a chemical cocktail mixed up for the propagation of the species. When the cocktail runs dry, you're just left with one hell of a hangover."

I start to wave my hand at myself then turn it to the affair couple as the perfect example. "Exhibit A."

Chloe doesn't turn to look, instead she stares at me. "Aunt

Erma must be paying you in gold," she says. She always was way too intuitive.

I shake my head. It's none of Chloe's business what Erma is paying me.

"I'm not naïve," she says. "No matter what you think. Yeah, I'm upbeat. I believe in silver linings and happily ever afters. That doesn't mean I'm blind to all the crap in the world. I just chose to be happy in spite of it. So yes. I'm sure. I'm going after my soul mate and I'm not going to give up until I find him. So here's my question for you. Are you in? Or are you out?"

I scowl at her fierce expression. Why do I feel like I'm leading a lamb to the slaughter? But if I don't go along, she'll do it by herself, and trouble follows her like a teenager with his first crush. I should know.

I pinch the bridge of my nose. I already agreed. I'm getting everything I want. There really isn't any downside to this. Just one week with Chloe and it'll be over. Really, there's no decision at all.

"I'm in," I say.

She grins. "I'll see you in the morning."

6

Chloe

SIX DAYS LEFT...

"I'M NOT RIDING IN THAT THING. NO WAY, NO HOW," I SAY.

That *thing* is a 1969 Dodge Charger. Think the *Dukes of Hazzard* car, except it's electric blue with a gray racing stripe. There's a dent in the passenger door, rust on the metal trim, and a long cut in the blue vinyl of the rear seats. The car roars when the engine turns and rumbles under you like a wild animal ready to be let loose. When it drives down a straight stretch you feel like you could soar to the moon, and when she's purring and still in a parking lot it feels like anything is possible as long as you lay down and soak in the splendor. The inside smells like gasoline and drive-in popcorn. Don't ask me how I know. This car and I go waaaay back.

"Shelly's not a thing. Don't hurt her feelings," says Nick. He strokes her hood lovingly and I resist the urge to throttle him. Figures that he still has her after all these years. He always did love her more than just about anything else in this world.

I'm not jealous. Puh-lease.

It's nine in the morning and it's time to head out on our cross-country road trip. My suitcase sits on the sidewalk next to me. It has my clothing, makeup, curling iron, toiletries, emergency chocolate, and my travel art supplies. Oh, and Veronica's survival kit. She insisted. All the essentials. I packed only my cutest and flirtiest dresses. I'm a dress girl as a rule, but I packed my best. There's no way I'm meeting my soul mate in anything less than a mega-flattering outfit.

"I can't believe you still own this thing," I say. I don't make a move to put my suitcase in the car. I'll start as I mean to go on, and I don't mean to go on in Shelly.

Nick runs his hands over the car's body. "Don't worry, baby, she doesn't mean it. She's just jealous of our special bond."

"Hello, Earth to Nick, we can't drive three thousand miles in this rust bucket. It was on its last leg in high school."

He gives me a dark look. "Put your bag in the trunk." He opens it for me.

I shake my head. "We can take my car," I say.

I point to my yellow Volkswagen Beetle. It's only two years old, I just had the oil changed, and most importantly, it can drive six thousand miles round trip without falling apart.

Nick turns to look at my car in its parking spot and starts to laugh. "Sparky. I can't drive that car."

I glare. "You won't be driving. I drive."

His shoulders shake he's laughing so hard.

"Done yet?" I ask.

"The backseat's not big enough," he says. Then he waggles his eyebrows.

Anger gushes up like that geyser Old Faithful. I'm steaming mad.

"You...you..."

"Use your words," he says.

"You'll never get in my backseat," I say. My voice rises and it sounds shrill, even to my ears.

He leans back against his car and chuckles, deep and wicked. "Couldn't fit. Looks too tight."

"Grrr...ack," I say. Great, he's reduced me to outraged animal noises.

Then, he picks up my suitcase and tosses it in his trunk, and before I can pull it back out, he's slammed the trunk shut.

"Nick. Nick." I tug at the latch, but it doesn't open.

He calmly walks to the driver door and gets in. Then he starts the car. It backfires and shoots oily black smoke at me. I jump back and cough. Nick rolls down his window and casually hangs his arm over the door.

"Come on, Sparky. The road's waiting. Your future of abject disappointment and betrayal lies just around the next bend. Hop in."

He. Is. Awful.

I bare my teeth and bite back a response. Calm is needed here.

I look up at the sky and ask heaven to send me a little help. It's mid-September and the sky is clear cerulean blue with a few wispy clouds. It's the kind of sky I'd paint on a card. The color alone reminds you of tart apples, hay rides, and the smell of falling leaves. Downtown Romeo is bustling. People pile in and out of the bakery with apple fritters, donuts, and their morning coffee. The toyshop and the bookstore are turning on their open signs. Mr. Kwan at the hardware store is watering his flower pots out front. I can hear the river running at the bridge and the old mill less than a block away. It's a perfect day in Romeo. After one last deep breath, my calm is restored. Thank heavens.

I walk over to Nick's open window and smile down at him.

"This car isn't road safe," I say in a reasonable tone.

He smirks. "Got her serviced last week. Greg at the garage said she's as fit as a fiddle. She'll make the trip no problem."

Unfortunately, Greg is my mechanic too, and I trust his judgment implicitly. I scuff my heel into the grass growing from a crack in the sidewalk. Okay, fine, the car's probably fine to make the trip. But it's more than that. I flick my eyes to the backseat. Nick notices where my eyes have travelled, and in a moment of surprising sensitivity, he looks away and gives me a moment.

Then, "I'm six foot four. I can't fit in your Bug. Shelly will get you where you need to go."

"But—"

He shakes his head. "She's never let me down. Not in fifteen years."

I look at the backseat again. It's smaller than I remember.

"I just...I don't really want to find my soul mate in the car where you and I...ugh."

He raises his eyebrows.

"Never mind," I say.

He nods and wisely doesn't say anything for a minute. Then, "You know. He could be in Connecticut, and that's only three hours from here. You'd be with your Matt Smith before lunch."

Good point.

"Okay," I say. "Fine. But don't think that I'm going to do anything just because I'm riding in your teenage love mobile."

I slide into the passenger seat and he flashes a grin my way.

"Shelly already worked her magic. I don't need a repeat performance."

"Creep," I say.

He shrugs. But there's color traveling up his neck and staining his cheeks. Oh my gosh.

"That's it, isn't it?" I ask. "That's the reason you're doing this. All these years you've been waiting to get back at me for breaking up with you. That's why you're here, you want another backseat performance."

He looks over at me and scowls. "Not even close," he says.

"Oh my gosh. Look at your face. You think you're going to seduce me away from my soul mate. That's how you're going to prove me wrong. That's why you're coming," I say. I'm floored.

His jaw clenches, then he yanks a picture from his pocket. "Think again," he says. He shoves a polaroid into my hands.

"What's this?" I ask. I look down at a photo of a bunch of trees and stumps.

"That is why I'm doing this," he says.

"For a tree stump?"

He grabs the picture and puts it back in his shirt pocket. "No. Not for a tree stump. You and your backseat fantasies have nothing to do with it. I'm here for this photo and nothing else."

Well.

I'm quiet as he drives out of Romeo and onto 87 South. The trees fly by. The first leaves are turning. Ochre yellow and burnt sienna are stark brushstrokes against the deep green of the roadside forest. Autumn in New York is a color artist's dream.

After an hour I look back at Nick. His jaw has unclenched and his hands are relaxed on the steering wheel.

"So, what was the photo of?" I ask.

He looks at me from the side of his eyes, measuring my seriousness. Finally, his shoulders loosen again. "It's ten acres out on the mountainside. I do this and the land's mine."

I consider this information. I remember Aunt Erma owns some vacant land outside of town that she never built on, but I didn't know Nick was interested in land.

"What for?" I ask.

He looks over at me and there's a soft look to his face that I haven't seen in a long time.

"When I was in the Marines, breathing dirt in the desert, sweating my ass off in the Middle East, all I could think of was this cool, quiet, shaded forest on a mountainside. It became my Eden." He looks over at me and scowls, like he's embarrassed to be caught dreaming of something.

"Oh," I say. "It sounds beautiful."

He stares out at the highway and I leave him be. I think about turning on the radio but remember that Shelly only gets the AM stations, so I leave it off. Two hours into the drive, I'm getting jittery. What if Nick is right and this is *my* Matt Smith? In an hour we'll meet and then...my whole life will change. I mean, it's likely that it's him. He's the only Matt Smith on the list that lives on the East Coast and this is where he grew up. It's probable that I'm about to meet the man that will love me forever.

I smooth my hands over my dress. It's a satin gown with an abstract watercolor pattern bursting with bright colors. It has little cap sleeves, a tight bust and a skin-tight skirt that hits above mid-thigh. I run my hands over the fabric and fuss with the skirt.

"Stop fidgeting," says Nick. "You're stressing me out."

My hands stop mid-stroke. "I guess it's good we didn't make it," I say. I clench my fists then loosen them. "We mix as well as oil and water."

He doesn't agree or disagree with my statement, which I was hoping he'd do. Instead he asks a question. "I always wondered, what would it take for you to know a guy was the one? Besides your aunt's say so."

I sink back into my seat and let the warm fuzziness of my romanticism settle around me.

"A grand gesture," I say.

He looks over at me and squints in the bright sunlight coming from my window. "What? Like running out on your wedding to be with the girl of your dreams?"

I wrap my arms around myself. "Don't be a dick."

"Sorry," he says, and...he means it. His voice is laced with regret.

"S'alright. Anyway, don't you watch romcoms?"

He turns and raises his eyebrows. "Do I look like I watch romcoms?"

I snicker. No. No he does not. But the way he says it, filled with dirty innuendo, makes me want to watch one with him.

"Fine," I say. I decide that I'm going to enlighten Nick on the highlight of the romcom. "A grand gesture is an elaborate and public declaration of love. It's a wedding proposal via sky writing airplane, or..." I shift in my seat, excited to be sharing my grand gesture theory. "It's organizing a serenade with a band and backup, where you sing a love song to prove—"

"Please. Stop." He shakes his head.

"What?"

"You're embarrassing yourself."

"What are you talking about? The grand gesture is a cultural icon."

He scoffs. "Riiight. The grand gesture. An icon for snivelly losers who can't get a girl on their own so they have to resort to emasculating themselves in some bizarre stereotypical ritual pre-ordained by out-of-touch romantics."

"That's not true! Some of the greatest love stories of all time have grand gestures."

Nick laughs. "Oh, right. I remember. Romeo kills himself. Juliet follows suit. Catherine dies. Heathcliff becomes a raving psycho."

"You read *Wuthering Heights*?"

"No."

I shake my head in confusion. "Those grand gestures weren't used for good. It's supposed to only be used for good, not evil."

Nick looks at me and lifts an eyebrow. "Wait. The grand gesture theory was invented in *Star Wars*? Spoiler alert, when Luke grandly blew up the Death Star and got the girl, he found out she was his sister. Grand gesture fail."

"Ugh, you're twisting everything around." I squirm in my seat and try to impress on him the importance of my belief. "Back to your original question. If my aunt hadn't told me my soul mate, I would've known he was the one by his grand gesture. And my ultimate grand gesture is a public love serenade Bollywood-style—big music, lots of color, singing, dancing, it would be the ultimate in romance." At least I think I would. Like I said, I haven't trusted my judgment in a long, long time. But still...

Nick sighs and looks at me like I've lost my mind. "You're lucky your aunt pulled the soul mate card. Because you'd never find a man willing to make a fool of himself like that. Not in a thousand years."

"Well, maybe you wouldn't—"

"I definitely wouldn't."

"So it's a good thing you're not my soul mate," I say.

"Damn straight."

"Fine."

"Fine."

I cross my arms over my chest and turn back to the window. Matt Smith lives only thirty minutes away. I let myself dream about what he'll look like, what I'll say when I meet him, how he'll fall into my arms and we'll be in perfect loving accord from day one. In my imaginings he's *nothing* like Nick O'Shea.

Besides, what could possibly be worse than a cynic like Nick?

7

Nick
Greenwich, CT
Matt Smith Number One...

THAT IS ONE BIG YACHT. REAL BIG. THE SUCKER HAS TO BE AT
least a hundred and fifty feet long. It's a shining white, polished
chrome, ginormous ode to penile one-upmanship. Matt Smith
Number One is hosting a party for feline Sphynx enthusiasts.
On his yacht.

It'd taken a little work to find this yacht. Number One lives
in a gated community for the mega rich, movie stars, and East
Coast elite. At least this is what the security guard told us when
he denied our entrance to the community. Regular Joes...not
allowed. Somehow Chloe managed to stupefy him with her
smile and before we knew it the butler was answering the door
of Matt Smith's waterfront mansion. The butler was very sorry,
but Matt was on his yacht at the harbor. Were we by any chance
here for the Sphynx gathering?

Why yes...yes we were.

The butler kindly gave us directions and here we are, staring up at the most massive yacht I've ever seen.

"He's my soul mate, I can feel it," Chloe says. She stands at the end of the dock and stares at the massive yacht, her eyes all sparkly and excited.

"Doubtful. The only thing I can feel is a hundred-foot-long inferiority complex."

She turns to me and beams, so I scowl at her.

"I don't care what you say. I have to get on that boat to meet my Matt Smith."

I step up next to her and look down at the gray, frothy water. It smells like fish, salt and seaweed, and there's some slimy green plant floating on the top. Not exactly pleasant, but hey, we won't be swimming in it. The yacht is moored a ways out, we're going to need to talk to the dockmaster for a tender boat to drop us off.

Chloe vibrates with anticipation. When we pulled up to the mega mansion, her eyes went wide with shock. But now...I expect she's going to start doing cartwheels down the dock.

She turns to me. Her cheeks are pink and her eyes are bright. "Remember in *Pride and Prejudice* when Elizabeth Bennet says she first realized she loved Darcy when she saw his huuuge estate?"

"No," I say. I cross my arms and stare at the huuuge yacht.

"Yeah. That moment." She grins at me and bats her eyelashes.

"Please, stop. Don't be the BBC made-for-television version of yourself," I say.

Her eyes widen and then she starts to laugh. "You watched it. You watched it! Nick O'Shea, Mr. 'I don't watch romance movies', saw *Pride and Prejudice*. This is amazing."

I glower as she does a little dance and fake boxes me.

"The more cynical they are, the harder they fall," she says.

I lift an eyebrow, a skill she always envied. "Not at all. I'm only trying to warn you."

"Oh, really?"

"Sure. This guy clearly has a major inferiority complex. He's making up for something."

She laughs. "Yeah right. You're just jealous of my soul mate's *big* yacht."

"Poor, deluded Chloe," I say.

"Poor, cynical Nick," she purrs.

I hold back a smile and nod toward the tender boat. "Come on," I say.

We take a quick ride out to the yacht. As we pull up, Chloe turns to me and I lean forward at the concern on her face.

"What is it?" I ask. I'll fix it if I can.

She pauses, then, "Please don't ruin this."

I step back, stunned. Is that what she thinks of me? I realize I'm clenching my jaw, so I relax and put on a smooth mask.

I don't say anything more because we're at Matt Smith's yacht—*The Hairless Jewel*.

I've never been on a yacht before, and if this one is typical, then I've been missing out. We step onto an expansive wood-floored deck, the bottom of three levels. There's two curving staircases with brass railings leading to the upper levels, plush white lounge chairs, umbrellas, a large circular hot tub, and...a sunburned man in a yellow speedo with thin legs and round knobby knees.

"Ahoy," he says. He waves at us and jumps up from his chair. He laughs and his banana hammock jiggles.

I knew it. There was no way a guy could own a yacht like this and be good looking.

"Inferiority complex," I say to Chloe.

She shushes me and smooths down her dress.

"Matt?" she asks.

"Ha. That's funny. No, I'm Carl. Cap'n Matt's just there."

He points behind him and we look to where he gestures. Chloe draws in a sharp breath.

You've gotta be kidding me.

A tanned man in a pink polo shirt, khakis and boat shoes walks toward us. I'm pretty sure music on the sound system starts up at his entrance. He's lady killer good looking. As he steps on the deck, the wind ruffles his hair and Chloe sighs.

Matt Smith smiles and Chloe tilts her head and sends a hundred watt smile back.

Matt Smith stutter-steps and then walks toward her with even more purpose. I fold my hands over my chest and glower.

"Matt Smith?" she asks in a hopeful voice.

He grins, and I note that he has the whitest teeth I've ever seen. "Why yes. Yes I am. And who may I have the pleasure of meeting? On my yacht's maiden voyage no less."

Chloe gives a small sweet giggle. I scowl harder and try to loom. I don't like this guy. And the more Chloe seems to like him, the less I do.

Number One takes her hand in his and presses a kiss to the back. I clench my jaw as he lingers and lingers. Chloe's cheeks flame red.

"He's not the one," I say. "Let's go."

She pulls her hand from Matt's and turns to glare.

"Stop it," she hisses.

She turns back to Number One, "I'm Chloe Daniels. I'm looking for my soul mate."

I want to slap my hand to my head. We really need to work on her delivery. But Matt Smith eats it up. He takes her arm and starts walking with her deeper into the yacht.

"Tell me more," he says. "I'm in favor of mates. Is there a test I can perform? To display my suitability?"

Whoa. "Not a chance," I say. I come up next to Chloe. She subtly kicks me with her heel. I sidestep her.

"Who's that?" asks Number One. He looks me up and down and then stands taller and wider.

"Oh, he's my—"

"Bodyguard," I say. I widen my stance too. I've got a good five inches on the guy.

Matt Smith takes this in. I send him a warning look. Apparently, I'm not frightening in jeans and an old The Strokes T-shirt from my garage band days.

Matt turns away and leads Chloe toward the interior of the yacht. We step onto lush white carpet and it sinks under my feet. The room has a high ceiling and wood paneled walls. There's plush white couches and chairs with fancy pillows, low wood tables, ottomans, pillows and tropical plants. At the far end is a white grand piano and a wood paneled bar with leather bar stools. Matt steers Chloe towards the bar.

"I'm hosting the Northeast Sphynx enthusiast annual gathering. The Sphynx are my life. I love them," says Matt Smith.

Chloe smiles up at him. "Lucky Sphynx."

Number One studies her and smiles approvingly.

"Do you know much about the breed?" he asks. Then he turns my way. "Your security can relax in the seating area." He waves at the couches. There are about a dozen high-society types dressed in resort wear and diamonds sipping martinis and talking in low voices.

Matt Number One gestures to a low couch that's unoccupied except for some animal that looks like a scrawny plucked chicken with a huge sparkling diamond collar.

"There's Cauliflower, my pride and joy," he says.

"Oh no. She's lost all her fur. The poor creature," says Chloe.

"Au contraire," says Matt. He leans closer and says in a low voice, "The breed goes au naturel. All the better to see them in their naked glory."

"Oh," says Chloe, although it comes out more like a squeak.

I don't hear Matt's response. He leads Chloe toward the bar. I sigh and sit on the couch, sinking into the plush fabric. I give this excursion about five minutes before Chloe realizes Number One isn't her soul mate. He's not right for her. She doesn't care about money, she needs a man to love her wholeheartedly. This guy's too wrapped up in his cats to give her the love she deserves.

The cat, Cauliflower, stands and performs a long stretch while it kneads its claws into the couch fabric. Its large ears are perked toward me and it stares at me with disconcerting blue eyes. It slowly picks its way across the couch toward me.

"What do you want?" I ask. I narrow my eyes at the cat.

It looks me up and down and then strolls the rest of the way across the couch. I look around the room. No one's paying me any attention. They're all engrossed in martinis and conversation. Chloe's at the bar with Matt. Cauliflower the cat puts its paws on my pants and looks up.

"What?" I ask. I'm not quite sure what it wants.

It keeps staring.

I shake my head. Okaaay. I reach out and scratch it under the chin.

"Meeeow rawr," it says. It sounds like an engine revving before a race. Then Cauliflower starts to purr and I swear she smiles at me.

Well, I'll be darned.

She kneads her paws into my pants and looks up. I'm no dummy, I get the cue. I scratch her under her chin a second time.

"Meeeow rawr," she says.

I think she likes me.

After she's done purring and kneading, she settles back and looks at me again. I get the pattern. I smile and scratch her under her chin. I guess cats aren't as bad as I always thought.

I pause for the meeeow rawr. Instead, Cauliflower vomits.

She pukes a golf ball-sized hairball all over my crotch.

"Gaaa," I say. I look at the hairball and then at Cauliflower.

"Meeeow rawr."

I jump up and swat at the wet slimy clump. "Are you kidding me?" I ask the cat. It looks like I peed my pants. I glance around the room. Nobody's looking my way. I cover the front of my pants with my hands and quickly walk out of the bar area back to the pool deck.

Carl is still lounging in his chair.

"Do you know where the bathroom is?" I ask.

"Door on the left," he says. "Looks like you got a little excited in there. Happens to the best of us."

I slink into the bathroom and splash water on my pants then scrub them down with the luxurious white hand towel. It still looks like I wet myself, but at least it doesn't smell anymore. It'll have to do.

I walk back into the posh bar room and sit on my couch. I check and see that Chloe's still at the bar chatting with Matt. Cauliflower meows and starts to prance toward me.

"No. Shoo," I say.

She jumps at the wet spot on my crotch and nuzzles her head into my pants.

"Off."

She holds on and claws at my pants.

"Off," I say.

Finally I manage to extract myself. It looks like Cauliflower reallllly wants in my lap, so I decide to head over and see how Chloe's getting on.

Matt's behind the counter of the bar looking through the refrigerated wine cabinets.

I come up behind Chloe and lean in close. I can smell her, that unique fresh-baked cookies mixed with watercolor paint that used to drive me wild. I move closer. "How's it going?" I say quietly.

"Eek." She jumps back into me. Her back hits hard against my front and I grab her waist and steady her.

"You startled me," she says.

Then she notices that she's plastered against me. Her backside to my front. We've not been this close in years. I can feel her curves pressing into me and the warm heat where we're connected. I clear my throat and try to move back.

"Sorry," I say.

The fabric of her dress tugs, but we don't come apart. There's something there, holding us together.

"Back up," she whispers.

I try again. I pull, her fabric tugs, and then we bounce back together.

"I can't."

She groans and wiggles her butt against me. I breathe heavily and clench my jaw. She rubs her backside back and forth. "Stop," I say. I grit my teeth. "Stop moving."

Matt pops back up with a triumphant grin and a bottle of champagne in his hands. His smile fades when he sees me. "Ah, hello," he says. "I was just retrieving a little bubbly. We were going to toast *mates*."

He looks at me as if this is my cue to leave.

"Ahh," I say slowly. "Aha."

"Wonderful, isn't it," says Chloe. She tries to pull away again, but just manages to wedge me closer against her.

Matt eyes me, looming over Chloe. She looks at her fingernails and hums. I yawn and look around the room.

"Do you need something?" asks Matt.

"Oh, he's joining us," says Chloe. She nods her head quickly.

Matt casts me a skeptical glance then pulls another glass down. "Very well." He sighs. "I was just describing to Chloe the act of feline mating."

"Aha," I say.

Matt holds the champagne bottle in his hands and runs his fingers down the neck of the bottle in a slow gesture. I take the opportunity to yank back. No go. Chloe rebounds into me. I grab her hips and stabilize her.

She squeaks and Matt looks up. Chloe fans herself. "Do go on. Please."

There's something holding us together. I just need to reach down between us and feel it. But how to squeeze my hand between my front and Chloe's backside?

"As I was saying, the male cat," says Matt, "seeks his female." He sends Chloe a meaningful look. "She's in heat and searching for her mate. Her scent drives him insane." Matt eyes Chloe's chest and runs his hands down over rim of the bottle.

I try to move my hand over her back, but Chloe kicks at me.

"The males will fight over the right to mount her," says Matt. He levels a look my way.

"Oh. Hmmm," says Chloe. "So, did you go to summer camp in Upstate New York?" Her voice is high and she wiggles her backside again. Too. Much. Rubbing.

"Stop," I hiss.

I finally feel the tiny space between us. There's a sharp pokey object with metal teeth stuck in the fabric of my pants and her dress. I try to tug at it, but it's not coming free.

"When the male mounts his female, he takes her from behind," says Matt. He pulls the metal wire from the cork.

"It was called Pine Hill," says Chloe in a desperate voice.

I try rotating my hips and shifting the fabric of my pants. The thing's not coming loose, but unfortunately, all this friction has caused something else to come up.

Not.

My.

Fault.

Chloe stiffens. "Are you kidding me?" she whispers.

"Not at all," says Matt. "The male cat has barbs on his penis. Upon copulation, the barbs sink into the female's vagina and keep the male stuck inside her until—"

I tug again.

"It was twenty years ago," says Chloe. "At Pine Hill Summer Camp."

I yank at the fabric, trying to break free of Chloe's backside.

"Can't get loose," I whisper.

"Exactly," says Matt. "The penis can't detach. Not until..."

Matt comes out from behind the bar to stand next to us. He forces the champagne cork from the bottle. It pops and I yank as hard as I can.

The champagne fizz rushes from the bottle head and spills over the rim. There's a loud rending of fabric as the back of Chloe's dress tears wide open. My arms pinwheel as I fall backwards. Chloe crashes into Matt. The bottle of champagne flies into the air and sprays bubbly liquid everywhere.

The entire back of Chloe's dress is open and she flashes her pink lace panties. She's on the ground and Matt is under her. Holy. Crap.

The room is silent.

No one dares to move.

Then Cauliflower hops onto the bar. "Meeeow rawr," she says. She begins to lick up the champagne.

From beneath Chloe, Matt Number One points at my wet pants. "Jewel thief," he sputters. "You're a jewel thief."

I gesture down at my wet crotch. "My jewels?"

Chloe rolls off Matt and clasps the back of her dress closed.

Matt jumps up. "You sicko. You're wearing my Cauliflower's jewels on your...your..."

I look down. Sure enough. Cauliflower's diamond collar is stuck to my zipper. So that's what was holding Chloe and I together.

Matt Number One yells louder and I notice the crowd of martini-drinking cat enthusiasts closing in. Not good.

Chloe is red faced and trying desperately to keep the back of her dress closed. I need to help her. But first I need to get this collar off.

"I'll have you arrested," says Matt.

I yank at it. The darned thing won't come off.

"Wait," says Chloe. I look up when I hear the panic in her voice. "Why are we moving?" I look back toward the pool deck. The shore is a good hundred yards away.

"You'll rot in prison," says Matt.

I tug again. I can't get the flipping thing off.

"It's a misunderstanding," I say. One thing I can guarantee, I'm not going to prison, not today and not tomorrow.

"Were you or weren't you at Pine Hill Summer Camp?" asks Chloe.

"I'll see you in court," Matt yells.

"Did you go to Pine Hill Summer Camp or not?" says Chloe.

"Not," says Matt.

Chloe looks stunned.

"Where are we going?" I ask. The shore is getting farther and farther away.

"Out to sea," says Matt Number One, "And then to prison."

Chloe and I look at each other.

"We've got to get off this boat," she says. "We've really got to get off this boat."

Uh. Yeah. We're not going to prison. Not for Matt Smith, we're not.

There's a wild spark in her eyes. The one that means she's determined to get what she's after and nothing's going to stop her. I used to love that spark.

"You coming?" she asks.

"First, let me detach," I say.

I drop my pants, leaving them and the jewels to Matt Number One. Then Chloe and I sprint to the brass railing on the deck. She climbs the railing and executes a perfect swan dive. Her head pops up as she treads water. The lunatic is grinning at me.

"Come on," she says.

I take one last look at Matt Smith chasing me down and leap into the water.

8

Chloe

IT'S TWO IN THE MORNING AND NICK AND I ARE JUST PAST Cleveland at a roadside motel. After swimming back to shore in the choppiest, fishiest water I've ever been in, we raced to the car. Then we grabbed our suitcases and took turns changing into dry clothes in the backseat. After that we hit up a gas station for wet wipes and new cell phones. Because, yes, swimming three hundred meters in salt water will ruin a cell phone. Luckily, credit cards are waterproof. We grabbed the cheap pay-by-the-minute phones and I thanked god that I had my parents', Aunt Erma's and Veronica's phone numbers memorized. I spent the blur of the next five hundred miles becoming even more determined to find my Matt Smith. Sure, the first try was a disaster. But there are five more to go and I have six days, well, five, left to find my soul mate.

There's nothing like watching the miles fly in a rumbly old Dodge Charger to get a person motivated. I have to admit, the way Nick sets his jaw and says we have five hundred miles to cover before we can rest makes me excited to take this trip with him. I never appreciated his discipline and his drive before today. Was it the military or was it always there? He laid out our stops and our timetable like he was planning a campaign. So, I watched the road, enjoyed the powerful car beneath me, and tried to ignore Nick as he sent glances my way and stroked his hands over the steering wheel. His fingers would run over the leather and I'd clench my legs together. He'd look at me while pretending not to look at me, then he'd move his hand to the shifter and gently circle his middle finger around the nub at the top. Gah.

No worries though. I'm on a mission, and my dark, handsome, sexy ex isn't going to stop me from finding my soul mate.

It took until the middle of the night, but finally we stopped for a rest.

"We have one room," says the teenage attendant at the motel front desk. He's behind a plexiglass window, and keys hang on a pegboard behind him. It's an old-school kind of place.

Nick stands next to me and I lean on the counter and rest my chin in my hand. Of course they only have one room. This wouldn't be a real road trip without the awkward hotel room sharing night.

"How close is the next hotel?" I ask. Maybe we'll get lucky and there's one down the street.

"S'all booked. Monster Truck Rally's this weekend," he says.

"So, like thirty minutes away?" I ask.

The clerk snorts, then pulls out his iPhone. "Grave Digger's here." He shows us a video of Grave Digger doing a flip. "There ain't no room for sixty miles."

Nick and I watch the video as the monster truck lands and spins in a circle around a stadium. "Wow. I've always wanted to ride in a monster truck," I say.

Nick shakes his head. "Unbelievable."

"Got mine out back," says the clerk. "She's a beaut."

"Yeah?" I ask.

"Take you muddin'" he says.

I lean forward. I've just come up with the best idea. "Would you buy a Valentine's Day card where a monster truck falls in love with the car he's supposed to crush?"

The clerk starts to laugh. "That's kinda sick, lady."

My shoulders sag. "Oh. I thought it was romantic."

"Unbelievable," says Nick again. "We'll take the room."

Which is how we find ourselves crowded into the entry of our twelve by twelve room. It smells like cigarettes and dry cleaning. There are water stains on the ceiling, cracks in the walls, a red vinyl chair, an oak desk and dark blue carpet with cigarette burns.

And..."That's one small blanket."

Nick laughs. "One small bed."

I walk slowly into the room. Nick locks the deadbolt and sets down our suitcases. We both take in the sight of the bed that's only slightly larger than a twin. He clears his throat and rocks back on his feet.

I rub my hands over my arms and remember that I'm covered in salt water and fish smell.

"I'm going to shower off," I say. I really want to get the stink of seaweed and fishy water out of my hair before going to sleep.

He relaxes and nods his head. "Take your time."

I close the door to the bathroom and lean against it for a

second. Then I turn on the shower. I try to be as quiet as possible. I suddenly feel more awkward than I have in my entire life. I'm undressing and Nick is maybe five feet away, separated only by the world's thinnest door. I hear the mattress squeak as he shifts on the bed. I imagine him stretching out and making himself comfortable.

I step into the shower and close the curtain. The warm water runs over my sore muscles and a long appreciative moan escapes.

"You alright in there?"

My eyes snap open and I cover my breasts with my hands. My heart pounds under my hands. But no. He's not coming in. He said it through the door.

"Fine," I say.

"Alright."

Jeez. My body's on high alert now. The rough sound of his voice through the door and the confirmation that he's *aware* of me send me into overdrive. I'm naked in here, and he's listening. Why doesn't that disturb me? Because it doesn't. I like it.

I close my eyes. Get a grip, Chloe. Been there. Done that.

But my body's not listening. There's tingling between my legs, my nipples are hard and the water running over them makes me want to moan again. The first time Nick pulled my top down he looked like he'd won the greatest prize in the world. Ten years later, I can still remember the feel of his mouth on me. I run the soap over my skin and relive the memories that I hide even from myself. There's the flash of his elusive smile. His dark eyes filled with belief in us rather than cynicism. My fingers tugging on his hair as he moves over my breasts and down. I draw my fingers across my nipples, over my ribs, down farther, until they're between my legs.

There.

I cry out. In my mind, it's his fingers twirling over my clit. He's the one teasing at my opening.

Nick. And dang it, I said that out loud.

There's a knock at the door. "Chloe?"

I squeeze my thighs together. "Thought I saw a spider," I call.

I can feel him standing at the door, like he's looking through it, considering my answer. Then, I hear the mattress squeak as he settles back onto the bed. I let out a breath and hit my head against the shower wall.

What am I doing?

Minutes later I'm in my pajamas. I wipe away the steam from the mirror and check my expression. I look normal-ish. No flushed cheeks, no embarrassed expression. Okay then. I pull open the door and step into the room.

Nick stretches out on the bed. "All set?" he asks. He avoids looking directly at me. I run my eyes over his long legs, his flat stomach and the bunching of his shoulders. There's a low heat flickering in me. It wouldn't take much for it to burst into flame.

"Good. I'm going to take a quickie," he says.

"What?"

But he's already jumped off the bed and closed the bathroom door. And now it's my turn to listen to the sounds of his clothing falling to the floor and the shower water running over his bare skin. I hear a low sound. My ears perk up. Is he...? There's a thud, then another sound, almost like a moan.

I stand and tiptoe to the bathroom door. My breath comes in short pants. The space between my legs feels heavy. I lean forward and rest my ear against the door.

The shower water's running. In my mind I picture him soaping himself up, running his hands over his...

"Dang, Chloe."

I jump back like a scalded cat and race to the bed. I yank the blanket back and dive in. Then I bury my head under the covers and wait for my cheeks to stop flaming and my heart to stop racing. In less than two minutes, Nick comes out of the bathroom. I peek at him. A cloud of steam follows him. He rubs his wet hair with a towel.

He's in boxers. Only boxers.

He's filled out since high school. Really filled out. Six-pack, bulky shoulders, biceps galore, narrow hips with muscled quads and calves. My lady parts clench in response to the massive amount of man on display.

I let out a long, slow breath. "I'll sleep under the covers," I say.

He shrugs. I watch as the muscles in his shoulders roll.

"Don't worry, Sparky. I'm not going to touch you."

"I know," I say. I turn the other way so he won't be able to see my expression, which probably says, *but I want you to.*

He climbs onto the bed and the mattress sinks under his weight. I involuntary roll toward him.

"Sorry," I say. I scoot back over to my half of the bed.

He sighs and reaches for the bedside lamp. He flicks it off and the room goes dark. Suddenly, this situation feels way too intimate. I feel the heat coming off Nick's body. I hear the steady sound of his breathing. Every movement he makes shifts the mattress and moves me closer in response. I even smell him, that fresh outdoor smell that sticks to him, apparently even after a shower. I slowly roll to my back and tilt my head toward him. My eyes are open and they start to adjust to the dark. There's a smoke detector with a small red light on the ceiling. I can make out Nick's outline, he's a darker shadow against the white sheets and the blanket. What would it have been like if Nick and I had stayed friends? Or, if somehow, we'd stayed together?

Except…no. He's not mine. We're not soul mates, and it would've never worked out.

"I can hear you thinking," he says.

"Really?" I ask. I'm glad to talk, it makes the situation less awkward.

"Are you thinking about Number One?"

"No."

"Number Two then?"

I sigh. "Sure."

He turns his head and looks at me through the darkness. His black eyes catch a flicker of the light and he searches my face, like he can see me better now than in the daylight.

"Don't worry, Sparky. You'll find him." His voice sounds sad, almost lonesome, but I think it's the darkness of the sparse hotel room and not anything he's actually feeling.

"Do you think after this we can be friends?" I ask. It's not something I've thought of until now, but I'm quickly realizing that I don't want to lose him again.

Then I want to kick myself, because even in the dark I can see his jaw clench.

"I don't want to *be friends*," he says. His voice is sharp and angry.

I flinch. "Sorry, I forgot. Nick and Chloe. Mortal enemies."

His whole body stiffens.

"You know," I say, "I have more reason to hate you than you do me."

There, I said it. Suck on that ball of sour.

He lets out a short, harsh laugh. "Yeah. Right."

"Why'd you even agree to be the substitute best man at my wedding?" I ask. It was shocking seeing him after so many years. Especially when he chose my wedding day to reappear.

"Does it matter? You'll think the worst no matter what," he says.

I shake my head. "Tell me anyway."

He's silent for a bit. I look over at the digital clock. Almost three in the morning. Three o'clock was always the time for secrets-sharing at my childhood slumber parties. I guess it holds true for adults too.

"Ron called. His best man, I don't remember his name—"

"Jeremy."

"Right. Jeremy backed out." He pauses. "I didn't know it then, but Jeremy knew about the affair. He didn't approve."

"Remind me to send a thank you card to Jeremy," I say.

"He likes monster trucks," says Nick.

"Was that a joke? Har har." I elbow Nick in the ribs, then pull back when I remember he's not wearing a shirt.

"Anyway. Ron called me up. He was desperate and I was already in town visiting my mom."

"I didn't know that. Do you visit a lot?" I can't imagine that Nick had been visiting Romeo all these years and I never knew about it. He ignores my question.

"Ron was a good friend in school and I felt some misplaced loyalty."

My ears perk up at his tone. "So, you didn't know about the..."

"No," he says. His voice is firm.

"Oh. I thought you did," I say. I feel guilty that I've been nursing a grudge.

"Nah. After we ate the wedding cake, I found Ron at the Holiday Inn and I—"

"You didn't."

I can feel him smile. It's glorious.

"Did you punch him?"

He doesn't answer.

"Put him in a headlock? Please tell me you gave him a wedgie and then dunked his head in the toilet. A dirty toilet."

"She's bloodthirsty," Nick says.

I laugh. "Oh my gosh. You did."

He laughs and I join him. My hero. Finally, I settle back into my pillow and gleefully imagine my ex-fiancé's toilet swirly. But something is niggling at me. Why would Nick bother?

"But why?" I ask. "You couldn't have cared that much."

Honestly, after the cake comment, I didn't think he cared at all.

"I came to the wedding to see the woman that haunts me tied in the chains of matrimony so she could never mess me up again. Ron ruined that for me."

Wait. What?

"What?" I ask out loud.

He stares up at the ceiling. "Go to sleep, Sparky."

"But—"

"Go to sleep. You've got a soul mate to find."

I let out a long sigh. He's right. Tomorrow, if we're lucky, we find Matt Smith of Chicago, Illinois. My would-be soul mate. I roll over and drift into a shallow sleep. I swear that during the night, I feel Nick's arms around me. My back is pressed into his chest and I'm warm and safe. But that can't be right, because in the morning, the bed's cold and Nick is sleeping on the floor.

9

Nick

SHELLY'S PURRING ALONG I-90 LIKE THE AWESOME CAR SHE IS. I pet her steering wheel just to make sure she doesn't feel any lingering hurt over Chloe's words. She's a good lady, my Shelly. I got her from a junkyard when I was fourteen and I worked on her for three years to restore her. Fixing her up kept me sane when my dad was driving us all into the ground. Shelly was my escape. After dad died and my family was left in piles of debt, I sold off everything I owned to pay Dad's debts, everything except Shelly. Then I went into the military so I could send my mom enough money to keep her and my kid sisters in our home, with food in the fridge. So, let's just say, Shelly and I have a bond. I know she's a car, but...I've told her things I never told anyone else. She's seen the lowest point of my life and the highest.

I look over at Chloe.

She's wearing another tight wrap dress. This one's pink with thin straps and a plunging neckline. My jaw clenches and I flex my hands on the steering wheel.

Not for me.

"You need to work on your delivery," I say.

Chloe is sipping a double pumpkin caramel latte with whip cream and sprinkles. I finished my no-frills coffee an hour ago. I take it black, because I don't trust cream or sugar. It hides the truth.

Chloe sighs. She's staring dreamily out the window at the turnpike north of Chicago. We're only fifteen minutes from Number Two's place. I repeat myself because clearly Chloe is stuck in a daydream about Number Two being the missing puzzle piece to the other half of her heart.

"You gotta work on how you deliver your line," I say.

"What?" she asks. She smiles at me, and I nearly swear. Now I know she's been dreaming about Number Two, because her eyes have gone all bedroom lusty on me.

"Pull it together," I say.

Her eyes snap out of the bedroom and back to reality. "You know, I like you a lot better when you aren't being so cynical."

I scoff. "Well, I like you a lot better when you aren't being such a delusional romantic."

I pull around a semi-truck and he taps his horn and salutes. I wave.

"You know him?" asks Chloe.

"He likes Shelly."

She takes another sip of her latte to cover a laugh. "I'd like her better if she had cup holders."

"When we meet Matt Smith today, you need to have a better

delivery," I say. "Don't just go..." I put on my high-pitched girl voice. "Hiii, I'm Chloe and I'm looking for my soul mate."

"What? I don't sound like that," she says.

"Yeah. Yeah you do."

"Okay, Mr. Know It All. If we didn't know each other and I came up to you, what would you want me to say?"

I stare straight ahead at the highway while Chloe waits for my response. The thought of Chloe coming up to me and telling me I'm her one true love...

"You wouldn't need to say anything," I say.

"Really?"

"Sure. If it's meant to be, then lightning will strike at that very moment and there won't be any doubt that we're destined for true love."

"Be serious. The chance of lightning striking us is—"

"One in seven hundred thousand. A better chance than finding your one fated love in a world of billions."

"Fine. I'll do it my way then," she says. She turns away and stares out the window.

A bitter taste is in my mouth. Probably the coffee. You see, I lie to myself sometimes. Unfortunately, I never believe me.

I signal and pull off the highway. We're headed into a town northwest of Chicago. It has a small-town Main Street sort of vibe. There are tidy lawns, maple trees along sidewalks, kids' bikes in front yards, and some wraparound porches. It looks like Number Two lives in a Norman Rockwell painting.

Chloe's going to love him.

I sigh.

She turns my way and shakes her finger at me. "You know what? I finally figured you out," she says.

"That so?"

"Yup. You're like the bitter dieter. You're all jealous that others are eating love buns and drinking love lattes while you starve yourself on black coffee and brussels sprouts."

"Brussels sprouts?"

"Yes. And guess what? Stop starving yourself. There's plenty of love to go around. Quit pressing your nose against my bakery window and find your own buns."

I can't help it, I start to laugh. Love buns?

"I've eaten plenty of buns," I say.

She snorts. "Uh huh. You're on a starvation diet if I ever saw one. I can tell when a dieter is raging and needing some sugar. You, Nick, are what happens when people don't let themselves eat the buns."

"I've eaten lots of buns," I say again, ignoring how ridiculous this argument sounds. It's the principle.

She shakes her head. "Nope. No buns. No sugar. No love."

"I love Shelly," I say.

"And I'm sure Shelly loves you back."

I swallow, then turn my head and pretend to check the directions on the pre-pay gas station phone. We're only two minutes away from Number Two.

"I'm sorry," Chloe says. She reaches over to put her hand on my arm. "I didn't mean—"

"We're here," I say. I look down at her hand and then up at her.

She pulls her hand away. "Nick..."

"If I were you, I'd have them tell you the name of the camp. Otherwise, how can you prove that they're the Matt Smith you're looking for? You wouldn't want to marry the wrong guy."

She searches my face and I itch under her gaze. "Alright. Okay," she says. She unbuckles and smooths her hands over her hair then down her dress.

I step out of the car and go around to hold the door open for Chloe.

We're in an upper middle class neighborhood. The type of neighborhood where the houses are elegant, the landscaping's professional, and flowers are planted for every season. Right now, the theme is orange and red chrysanthemums. Chloe steps out of the car and onto the sidewalk. She's in a pair of high wedges and her legs look a mile long.

We stop and stare at the tall stately white colonial in front of us. There's a flag that says "Welcome" on the front porch and ceramic pots with flowers.

"If you like Hallmark Channel towns, this is the place for you," I say.

"I love the Hallmark Channel," Chloe says.

Yeah, I kind of figured. She nibbles a bit on her nail, her nervous tic, and then squares her shoulders. "Hi, I'm Chloe. We could be soul mates."

"Talking to yourself?" I ask.

"Shh. I'm practicing."

I chuckle.

We climb the front porch steps. There's a porch swing, some Adirondack chairs and a welcome mat. This place has a lot of charm. Chloe knocks on the glossy red front door. I rock back on my heels and shove my hands into my pockets. No answer. Chloe knocks again. There's no noise coming from the house.

"I don't think he's home," I say.

"Shh," says Chloe. "I heard something." She knocks harder.

"No, he's not—"

I stop, and a chill runs down my spine.

Chloe whips around.

That was a scream. Someone inside the house screamed.

"Did you hear that?" she asks.

I nod. Chloe's face goes white. The screaming starts again. Long and shrill, then "Help me! Help me!"

"He's killing her. My soul mate is killing someone." Chloe starts pounding on the door with the side of her fist.

There's loud thuds in the house and it's possible that a large piece of furniture was knocked over. There's another scream and another thud.

Chloe spins toward me. "Nick. Open the door. Call the police. Do something." She kicks the door and pounds it again. She's frantic.

I shake my head.

"I don't think we should go in there," I say. "I don't think we should interrupt."

She rounds on me. Her eyes are wild and she looks like she could take me down in a second. "Nick O'Shea, open the freaking door right now. Open it."

I hold up my hands. "Alright. Whatever you say."

I try the door. It's a simple lock that won't be any trouble to break.

"Hurry up. Can't you hear her?" Chloe grips my arm and her fingernails dig into my skin.

"You sure?" I ask again.

"Do it."

I grab a credit card from my wallet and slide it between the doorjamb and the lock.

Fifteen seconds of jimmying and it pops open. The front door swings wide. Chloe pushes around me.

"We've called the police..."

Then she focuses on the woman lying at the base of the stairs. It's gruesome. It's possibly one of the messiest scenes I've ever witnessed.

"Not...not..." Chloe says. She grabs her stomach like she's going to be sick.

"Now that's a love bakery."

The woman who was screaming is covered in melted ice

cream, whipped cream, donuts and...girl scout cookies? There's a man above her with his hairy butt cheeks bared. He whips around.

"Who the hell are you?" he yells.

The woman shrieks and scrambles behind him. The man doesn't have any problem with us seeing his bits and pieces.

"Matt Smith?" asks Chloe in a dazed tone.

She can't tear her gaze from the waffle cone held in place by a licorice string covering his...yeah.

I grab Chloe, slowly back out onto the porch, and slam the door after us.

10

Nick

WE'RE HAVING HOT TEA IN THE KITCHEN. THERE ARE HENS AND roosters on the border wallpaper and a ticking cuckoo clock on the wall. It just cuckooed twelve.

"Do you take milk?" asks Rachel. She's all cleaned up and in an orange pant suit.

"No thanks," I say. I take a sip of the scalding hot black tea from my china cup. It clatters and some tea spills over the edge into the saucer when I set it back down.

All four of us are seated around the kitchen table. Everyone is drinking tea with pinkies in the air, trying with all our might to pretend that the previous meeting didn't happen. If we act as decorous as the Queen, then clearly none of us saw a waffle cone penis and maraschino cherry nipples.

"I'll take milk, please," Chloe says.

Rachel pours milk from the tiny ceramic cow pitcher.

"Thank you," Chloe says.

"You're so welcome," Rachel says.

I swallow another gulp of the tea and wince when it burns my tongue. The man, Ernest, makes a sour face. He has smooth, small hands that fit perfectly with the delicate cup he holds.

"You know my cousin Matthew, then?" he asks.

"Yes," Chloe says. She clears her throat and sets down her cup. "We drove all the way from New York to see him. We're very sorry to barge in on you...I mean...um...I'd be so grateful if you could tell us how to find him?"

Ernest gives a short laugh that is somewhat reminiscent of a hen clucking. When he stops he shares a look with Rachel. It's the kind that's loaded with three months' worth of conversation. I take another swallow of the tea. It's bitter without milk or sugar.

"You see..." Chloe says.

I narrow my eyes. Oh boy. I can tell she's gearing up for the soul mate line. Her eyes have gone all dreamy and she's leaning forward earnestly.

"We have a bequest that was left for him," I say.

Chloe turns sharply to me.

"Oh my," says Rachel. Her hands flutter and pat the pearls at her throat.

Ernest clucks and shakes his head. "A bequest?"

"From a mutual friend," I say.

Chloe kicks me under the table. Too bad she's wearing wedges and cork heels don't hurt.

"Oh, well, isn't that wonderful?" says Rachel. "We've had so many people skulking around asking after Matthew."

"Really?" I ask.

She nods. "Unsavory types. Not the type you'd invite to tea."

"Ah," I say. I take another sip of tea, just to make sure we're all on the same page. I, Nick O'Shea, am a man you'd invite to tea.

"Oh, we'd never skulk," says Chloe. "We just need to find Matthew so he can have his happily ever after. We all deserve our happily ever afters. Don't you think?" She folds her hands in front of her and her smile is full of hearts and sunbeams.

A sparkling ray of light shines through the window and lands on her pink cheeks. And I swear, birds start to sing.

I glance at Ernest and Rachel and they are eating up this Disney moment.

Unbelievable.

She *nailed* her delivery.

I cannot freaking believe it.

"Oh that's wonderful, isn't that wonderful, sweetums?" says Rachel.

"Sure is, sugarplum," says Ernest.

"So, you'll tell us where Matt is?" Chloe asks.

Rachel takes Ernest's hand and squeezes. Her face softens and she smiles at the both of us. Suddenly, I've got a real bad feeling about this.

"Certainly," says Rachel. She leans forward and Chloe leans in too.

"Where is he?" Chloe asks.

"Not too far," Rachel says. "Matthew's in prison."

11

Chloe

MATT SMITH NUMBER TWO, TAKE TWO

SO, IT TOOK A LITTLE CONVINCING TO GET NICK TO AGREE TO visit the correctional facility where Matt's being held. Let's just say, he was not enamored with the idea. But here's my argument...a soul mate doesn't care what's in a person's past. They love them *in spite of*. That's the deal. In spite of.

If I'm ready to marry a bazillionaire that owns a yacht and a mansion, then I can be ready to marry a guy in prison. That's how this thing works. You don't get to choose your fated one. You just get to love them.

Nick got a little cold-eyed and cranky at my reasoning, but he finally agreed. It's sort of funny, I never used the "in spite of" argument for Nick. I wonder if I'd be able to forgive our past and practice "in spite of" with him? Doesn't really matter, it's a moot point.

Anyway, I'm counting on the "in spite of" to work in my favor too. I haven't had much luck with men loving me all the way, one hundred percent in the past. But with soul mates, they love you in spite of all the flaws you have.

We roll up to the guard booth at the facility. I've never been to a prison before. There are two tall fences with barbed wire spaced about ten feet apart surrounding the whole facility. I guess, if a prisoner jumps one they still have another fence to clear. There's a tall guard tower, sort of like an airport tower. Finally, there's the prison itself, which depressingly, looks similar to most of the 1950s ugly orange brick schools found all around the U.S.

We provide our IDs and state the reason for our visit. Then a German shepherd sniffs our car. Finally, we're cleared to pull into the visitor lot. We're in luck, it's an approved visiting day and hour.

Maybe it's a sign from the universe.

"Let me do the talking," says Nick.

"I'll be fine," I say.

Nick's been all growly and alpha protective on me ever since Rachel and Ernest said Matt's a convicted criminal. Sure, I freaked out for a millisecond, but if it's meant to be, it's meant to be. If not, we'll move on.

I go to jump out of the car, but Nick holds out his hand. "Sparky, wait."

I pause and really look at Nick. His jaw clenches as he looks at the entrance to the prison. "This isn't going to be all hearts and rainbows," he says. "This guy could be a real psycho."

"Or a lumberjack," I say.

He cuts his hand through the air. "This isn't a joke. We're at a prison. If you keep on your insane mission to find your soul mate you could get hurt. Not all people have your best interest at heart." He turns to me and I take in the earnestness of his expression. "Not all people are good, Chloe."

Wow. He's really freaked out. I reach out and touch my fingers to the warm skin of his forearm. Slowly, the tension leaves and he relaxes beneath me.

"I'll let you do the talking," I say.

He closes his eyes and lets out a long breath. "Thank you."

"But if he's my soul mate," I say.

When he opens his eyes I flinch back. There's an ache there. A broken, hurting ache. I don't understand...why should this bother him? He knows what this trip is about, and he knows how it will end.

"Nick?"

He shakes his head and the look in his eyes vanishes. "Let's get this over with," he says.

It takes nearly an hour to go through security and check-in. Finally, after two cups of stale vending machine coffee, it's go time.

Nick and I sit down at one of the metal and Formica-topped tables. I hold my Styrofoam coffee cup in my hand. The room is about the size of a small cafeteria. There are other prisoners talking with their guests. A number of guards watch with jaded eyes. The walls are grayish-green, the floors are light gray gymnasium linoleum, and there's an instructional poster on the wall. The room smells almost exactly like a school gym.

I shift on the hard seat. Then, the door opens and a stern-faced prison guard escorts in a prisoner.

Matt Smith.

He's shorter than I imagined. And nicer looking. I mean, he looks friendly. He's short and has a round boyish face. He studies us with some curiosity, but not much. I reach for that bolt of lightning, or at least for some sort of sign that he's the one, but nothing happens. Do I feel drawn to him?

Matt notices my eyes running over him. He cocks his head and winks.

"Hey, pretty lady," Matt says.

Nick stiffens. "Nope," he says.

"Pshaw," says Matt.

After he takes a seat he leans back and spreads his legs. It looks like he's settling in for a long, relaxing chat. Except then he starts cleaning the nail of his pointer finger with this thumbnail. I glance at Nick, and he quirks an eyebrow at me. Yup, Matt Smith is ignoring us.

Nick clears his throat. "You're Matt Smith?"

"What's it to you?" Matt doesn't look up from his nail-cleaning.

Nick stares at me and I can tell what he's thinking...*time to go*.

"Hi there, I'm Chloe."

Matt stops cleaning his nails and looks up at me, then Nick. "Who's that?" he asks.

What did we say last time?

"My brother," I say.

"Her boyfriend," says Nick.

"My brother's boyfriend—"

"Boyfriend," says Nick.

Matt nods sagely. "Got one of those, too."

"Mmmhmm, exactly," I say.

"We have some questions," says Nick.

"Nah, man. Not interested."

Nick turns to me and nods his head toward the door. "Let's go."

Clearly, he thinks that this Matt isn't the one. But I need to be sure.

"Did you ever go to summer camp in New York?" I ask.

Nick gives me his hard stare. I glare back. I'm not going to mention soul mates, jeez.

"Course," says Matt.

Oh. Wow.

Nick swings back to him. "What did you say?"

Matt shrugs. "Course I did."

I think Nick's about to jump over the table and throttle Matt into taking it back. I ignore Nick and lean forward. *This is it.* My soul mate is here. In prison. Across from me. Right now.

My stomach rolls and I press my hand into it.

"Do you remember its name?" I ask. My voice shakes. I think I'm going to be sick, right here on the ugly Formica table.

"He didn't go," says Nick, his lip curls in a sneer. "He's messing with you."

"Pshaw," says Matt. "Am not. Went there every summer, worked on my music." His face transforms into pure happiness as he starts to hum a tune.

"Oh, you're an artist," I say. "Me too."

"Chloe," says Nick in a warning tone. But I won't be prejudiced against Matt. If he's the one...it'll all work out. I trust that soul mates are real, and I trust it with my whole heart.

Matt sits up straighter. "That's right, pretty lady. I had a record deal. Toured the U.S. My band's waiting for me in LA. They got gigs lined up out the..." He trails off when he sees the expression on Nick's face.

"So you're a musician?" I ask. I nod my head and give Matt a big smile. "I love music."

"Music's my life, yeah? That's why prison's hell." He looks down at his hands and rubs the pads of his fingers, like he's feeling for old calluses.

"Why?" I ask.

"Can't feel the beat here," he says. He squeezes his hands together and drops them to his lap. "It got taken away." His boyish face appears older.

I look around the stark, institutional room at the oppressive gray and the heavy weight of the walls. I've always believed there's something to be thankful for, no matter what, but right now, I'm not sure what to say. I imagine how I'd feel if I couldn't draw or paint anymore.

"The color's gone," I say. "All gone."

Matt takes in the expression on my face. "You get me," he says.

"What are you here for?" I ask.

"Fraud."

"What did you say the camp was called?" asks Nick.

I pick up my coffee and take a slow sip.

Matt shrugs. "Eh. I don't know. Pine something."

I spray my coffee across the table. It shoots out of my mouth in a violent stream and hits Matt in the face. He jumps back.

Nick swears.

"Sorry," I say. "Sorry."

I swipe at the coffee splattered over the table.

"I'm so sorry," I say again.

Matt wipes at his face. "Nothing wrong with exchanging bodily fluids."

"No," says Nick in warning.

A guard moves our way. "Is everything okay, ma'am?"

"Sorry, I accidentally choked on my coffee."

He nods and moves back toward his station near the door.

"What was the camp called?" I ask. "Pine..."

I stare at Matt. I feel like a deer caught in headlights. There's an oncoming collision but I can't look away and I can't get out of the road.

Matt's oblivious to my internal freak out.

This is it. He's probably my soul mate. I look over at Nick. There must be something in my face because his eyes get fierce and his jaw hard. Then he shakes his head and starts to stand. He grabs for my hand and nods to the door.

"Come on. We can go," he says.

That's when I realize he's giving me an out. If I'm too scared or don't want this, Nick will pull me out of here right now and we'll both pretend this never happened. For me, he'll drive back to New York and tell everyone that we checked everywhere but never found my fated one. He's trying to protect me...but... "I have to do this," I say.

Nick stiffens and I feel a change come over him. His hand tightens on mine and he studies my expression. "You're sure?" he asks in a low voice. His two words carry a load of meaning, but I can't decipher them. What is he asking, exactly?

Matt doesn't notice. He's smiling at the ceiling. "I loved those days, man. Good old Pine...Pine..."

I pull my hand from Nick's. "I'm sure," I say to him.

A coldness falls over his gaze and he lets me go. He sits down.

"Pine?" he asks.

"Pine River," Matt says, "In Utica."

All the anticipation and confusion evaporate. I'm back again, sitting on a hard seat in a prison, with a stranger who shares the name of my soul mate but isn't mine.

It's not him.

Nick leans back and moves farther away from me. He glances over and there's an ironic twist to his lips. "Pine River," he says.

"Those were the good days," says Matt.

I shake out of my reflections and turn back to Matt Smith. It could've been him. It's not, but it could've been.

"It was nice meeting you," I say. "I hope you can find music again—" I stop.

Nick scowls at me and shakes his head like he's disappointed in me. Like in this moment, I've failed to be the person he thinks I am. The look hurts and I don't know why. I sit back down.

"I was in a band," says Nick.

I do a double-take. How did I not know this? But Nick's ignoring me.

"Yeah, man? What'd you play?"

Nick shrugs, "Drums. Badly."

Matt Smith snickers. "You gotta be okay sitting in bad for a long time before you get to good."

"Yeah," Nick says. "I never made it to good."

Matt settles back in his chair and nods in understanding.

"How's this?" Nick says to Matt. He starts to tap his hands on the tabletop. It's a quick, rhythmic beat, and then he starts to hum.

I stare. This is a side of Nick I've never seen. He's refusing to look at me, instead he's facing Matt Smith.

"You got it?" he asks.

"Yeah, man. Yeah. That's beautiful," Matt says.

Nick shrugs and keeps up the beat.

Matt starts to hit his fingertips on the tabletop. Then he starts to sing. "*All day long they work so hard, til the sun is going down, working on the highways and byways wearing a frown, you hear them moaning their lives away,*" sings Matt. He has a voice of pure gold.

After a moment he stops singing and looks at Nick. "Awww man," he says. "Thank you. You guys needed something?"

"No," says Nick. "It's alright."

"Anything you need," says Matt.

Nick nods. "We'll see you around."

Nick stands and holds out a hand for me. I take it and then pull back just as quickly. There's too much feeling there when I touch him. We walk out of the prison in silence. I'm confused. I don't understand the emotions under the surface and I don't get what he did in there.

When we make it to the parking lot, I turn to him. "Hey," I say.

Nick's shoulders stiffen but he keeps walking. His strides eat up the distance to the car. We make it back and he shoves the car key into the passenger door lock.

"Hey," I say louder. He ignores me, so I nudge at his back. "Hey."

"What?" he asks. He yanks open the door.

"What was that?" I ask.

He swings around, and I take a step back at the expression on his face. He's angry. Really angry.

"What was what?" he asks coldly.

I wave my hands toward the prison. "That. You signed on to help me find my soul mate. Why do you keep trying to prevent it from happening?"

"Are you kidding?" he asks.

"No. Why would I kid? What's wrong with you?"

He paces the length of Shelly and back again. "Nothing. Absolutely nothing. Only I just realized the girl I've known since I was two years old would rather marry a stranger who's spending the next fifteen years in prison than walk away with me. You'd choose a convict you don't know over..." He stops pacing and faces me. "I forgot life's ultimate truism—people always disappoint you in the end."

I stare at him in shock. He runs his hand through his hair and swears long and low.

"But what about the song? What about what you did?"

He turns away. "I don't know, Chloe. I was trying to give him a little light in that dismal place." He gestures to me and I look down at my bright pink dress and high heels. "You prance in there looking like a magical rainbow and then you prance right out again, not caring about the empty wreck you leave behind. Let me tell you, it sucks to be left behind. I was giving him something to have rather than the memory of your back." His mouth twists into a bitter line, and then he turns away from me.

I try to articulate a response but I can't. Finally, I manage to say, "I can see how it might've come across."

He shakes his head. "This isn't a game. These guys are real people."

"I know that." Tears gather in my eyes. I'm not sad, I'm frustrated. Really, really frustrated. I see where this is coming from. I step up to him. "You had your chance," I say. "You blew it."

He flinches. "That's not what this is about."

"Really? Isn't it? There was a time I thought you were *the one*." A tear falls on my cheek and I swipe it away. "I would've followed you in a car, to a prison, or across the world. Anywhere. But you blew it."

"If I'd known you'd have such high standards for your first lay, I would've practiced more. But don't worry, Sparky, I've improved with time."

I gasp. "You've got your head up your butt."

I turn away and get into the passenger seat, sealing myself away from him.

Nick stands a moment with his hands on the hood of the car and his head bent. Finally, he gets in and turns the key until Shelly revs to life.

"For what it's worth," I say, "I would've forgiven you anything but that."

I remember the day after we had sex. How much the *after* hurt.

He pulls out of the parking spot.

"It's funny," he says, "back then, for what it's worth, I would've forgiven anything. Full stop."

I turn away from him.

Next stop, Nebraska.

12

Nick

Four Days Left...
  Matt Smith Number Three

We're in Lincoln, Nebraska at the medical office of Doctor Matthew Smith. It's a little after nine in the morning and the office just opened. Doctors' waiting rooms are funny. They've got vinyl chairs that can be sanitized easily, laminate counters that can be sanitized easily, and magazines that carry all the germs in the place.

I grab a *Popular Mechanics* and flip through it while Chloe talks to the receptionist. We had a five-hundred-mile drive to cool down and get over the Number Two incident. It was my bad, I shouldn't have reacted the way I did. I know Chloe, and one of the best things about her is her certainty and purpose. She decides something, and then she does it. Don't get me wrong, I still don't believe in soul mates, I give human free will a little more credit than that, but I have to give Chloe her due for sticking to her beliefs.

Maybe by the end of this she'll chuck nearly thirty years of romanticism, but I doubt it. I'm starting to realize that I care more about making her happy than making her see she's wrong about love.

I glance at her. She's leaning on the receptionist counter, an earnest look on her face.

"I really need to speak to the doctor for a moment," she says.

"Does your husband need an appointment?" asks the receptionist.

"Who?" asks Chloe.

The receptionist lowers her glasses and stares at me.

"We're not—"

"He's not—"

"Your husband needs an appointment to speak with the doctor. He has a cancellation and can see you at ten." The receptionist holds out a clipboard. "Fill these out, I need ID and insurance."

"But it's not a medical issue," says Chloe. "I just need to ask him a quick question." She ignores the clipboard that the receptionist is waving at her.

The receptionist drops the clipboard and eyes me. "Sir. All questions for the doctor require an appointment."

"Excuse us a minute," I say. I pull Chloe to the side wall near the Purell dispenser. "Just make the appointment."

She shakes her head. "I don't want to be in a hospital gown or something when I ask him if he's my soul mate."

Her face is pinched and pale. "Are you afraid of doctors?" I ask.

"No, don't be silly, that's completely—"

I raise an eyebrow.

"Accurate," she says. She lets out a long breath. "Yes, okay. I'm terrified of doctors."

I try to hold back a laugh, but a little huff slips out.

"It's not funny." She pushes my arm, but she's such a lightweight I barely feel it. "They have gloves, and weird masks, and they..." She waves her arms around.

"They?"

She sighs. "They give bad news."

I remember now that when she was eight her dad was diagnosed with non-Hodgkin's lymphoma. Chloe was there for the bad news. He survived, but...I get it.

"I'll do it," I say. "I'll make the appointment."

"Really?" she asks in a hopeful voice.

"Yeah. You keep saying I'm trying to sabotage you, but I'm not."

She gives me a small smile. "You are, too. Anyone that didn't have their head up their butt could see it."

I wink at her. That was an apology for yesterday if I ever heard one.

"Harsh, Sparky. But I'll show you. I'll do whatever it takes to find your Matt."

She looks surprised, but hadn't I already committed to this job back in Romeo?

I walk back to the receptionist. She's typing on her computer and ignoring me.

"I'd like to make an appointment," I say.

She picks up the clipboard full of paperwork and gives me a knowing smile. "Good. Sometimes you men take a little coaxing. I see it all the time. What's your complaint?"

"Um," I look back at Chloe. "Pain."

"Okely-dokely. Fill out these forms and they'll call you when the doctor's ready."

I sit down in a vinyl waiting room chair and start to fill out the twelve pages of history and consent forms. I'm not really paying too much attention to them. Chloe sits down next to me and leans close.

"Thanks for doing this," she says.

I shrug and keep scrawling on the pages. "It's not a big deal."

But I can tell it is. Her eyes keep shifting nervously to the door to the back.

"You can hope this Matt isn't the one. I won't tell," I say.

Chloe waves my suggestion away.

An old man with frizzy hair sits down next to me. For a full five minutes he stares at me. I shift in my seat and try to ignore him, although it's really hard not to feel uncomfortable when someone keeps looking at you.

Finally he leans across me to talk to Chloe. "Who y'all seeing?"

"Oh." She turns to him. "Dr. Smith. Do you know him?" She pauses. "Is he nice?"

The old man's face splits into a huge wrinkled smile. "Nice? You could say that. Around town we call him The Cucumber."

I cough into my fist. "What did you say?"

Chloe cuts off a laugh.

"The Cucumber." He looks at me and winks.

"Like, baby gherkin kind of cucumber?" asks Chloe. "Or the big baseball bat kind?"

Unbelievable. The doctor is so famous for the size of his schlong that even the senior citizens have heard about it.

"Is this your first exam?" the old man asks me.

"Yes," I say.

He smiles again and leans back in his chair with a sigh. "Then you'll be seeing what I mean real soon."

Chloe turns to me with wide eyes. What the...?

I scowl at the man. "With all due respect, you shouldn't accost perfect strangers with tales about a doctor's *cucumber*."

The man's face turns red and then he starts to laugh in a long whiny wheeze. "I'm talking about his finger. His finger."

I have no idea what to make of that. The door to the back opens and a nurse calls out, "Mr. O'Shea."

Chloe and I both stand and walk to the back. In the room, I change into a blue gown with ties to the back. Chloe sits in a chair in the corner. I look around the room at the medical posters on the walls, the anatomy models on the counter, and the instruments set out on a metal tray. I swallow. Hard.

"Do you notice a theme?" I ask.

She looks at the posters and the models. "Ummm."

There's a wide display of butts, rectums, and arseholes. You get the idea.

"He's a proctologist," I say. I sit down on the exam table and plaster my bare bottom to the cold paper. These cheeks are not moving.

"How did I not know this?" I ask. His sign said Matthew Smith, M.D., not Matthew Smith, M.D., explorer of rectums.

Chloe must see my panic because she stands and points at me. "You said you'd do this. You said you'd help me find my Matt."

"That's before I knew he was a proctologist."

"Please, Nick."

I shake my head. She folds her hands in front of her.

"You don't have to do anything but lay there. I'll ask my question right away," she says.

I stare at the wall in front of me. There's a row of latex gloves. Small. Medium. Large. None of the small or medium boxes have any gloves removed. The large box is almost empty. My world zooms into that one box. Large gloves mean large hands. *Cucumber* hands.

"I can't do this. No way."

The door swings open. A tall man in a white coat walks in reading from a clipboard.

"You must be Nick," he says without looking up.

He turns his back and washes his hands in the sink. I try to scoot forward to get a look at them, but I can't see around his wide back.

"Uh...yup," I say.

"What are you here for today?" he asks.

He turns. I look down. He's wiping his hands with a paper towel so that I still can't see them. How big are they? I look over at Chloe. Can't she ask him already? She sends me a pleading look. I turn back to Dr. Smith.

"Pain," I say. Pain in the butt.

He finally drops the paper towel into the trash and his hands are revealed. My mouth goes dry. The old man was right. At least I think he was. I've lost the ability to ascertain a hand's normal size.

"Can you describe the pain? Dull, sharp, persistent?"

I can't look away from them. I back up on the table. "Persistent. Definitely persistent. What do you say, Chloe? Would you say persistent?"

I turn to her and realize she's staring at his hands as well. "Enormous," she says, like she's in a freaking trance.

"Chloe, didn't you have a question for the doctor?"

She shakes her head and snaps out of it. "Dr. Smith, did you ever go to summer camp in New York?"

He chuckles and reaches for the wall of latex gloves. I watch as he pulls out two large gloves.

"You're a New Yorker, too? I thought I heard an accent. That's excellent. Now just lay on your side for me, facing the wall. We always do a physical exam on the first visit."

Oh, no. I send Chloe a beseeching look and move my hand in the wrap it up gesture.

"I am. I'm from Romeo. Did you go to summer camp in upstate?"

"Lay down, please," says the doctor.

I watch as he picks up a long tube and squirts a glob of lube on his finger tip. He moves forward, I can feel him near. I flip and smack my butt to the table.

"Chloe," I say.

"There's some lovely camps in New York," she says. "Did you ever go to one as a kid?"

"Now roll over, this only takes a second," he says.

Chloe sends me another pleading look. I turn again on my side. The things I do for this woman. What wouldn't I go through?

"Hmmm, upstate camps," says the doc.

I feel his finger coming at me again. I flip on my back.

"This isn't going to hurt," he says in a stern voice. "Just relax and lie on your side."

"Please, Dr. Smith," says Chloe, "I really need to know. Were you ever at camp in upstate New York?"

He grunts, and then, "No, can't say I was."

Thank the lord, it's over. I move to get off the table. But right when my guard's down the doc sneaks in and...

"Yaaaa grrr jeez," I say.

I flinch and tense up.

"Breathe. Relax," he says in a calm voice.

I am relaxed. I'm always relaxed. I'm the most relaxed person I know.

"Sorry," squeaks Chloe.

She sounds mortified and suddenly I'm in a great mood. I have an idea...

"Hey, Doc," I say.

"Yes?"

"You find my head up there?"

He grunts. "No. Can't say I did."

I lay on my side and grin.

"Hear that, Chloe? My head's definitely not up my butt."

13

Chloe

SINCE THIS IS MY FIRST CROSS-COUNTRY ROAD TRIP, I WASN'T prepared. There are weird things that happen when you travel thousands of miles on the same road. We've been on I-80 for nearly fifteen hundred miles. The road becomes a hypnotic blur, and the long flat stretch of Illinois, Iowa, and Nebraska refuse to offer any distraction. There was even a stretch of three hundred miles where there were no coffee shops, which means I didn't have a single latte to distract me.

Which leads to the weird thing. Sitting in a tight space with Nick O'Shea for *thousands* of miles makes me antsy. Very antsy. I've tuned out the road and become aware of him. I've started to memorize his movements again, and his gestures, and his expressions. I can tell whether he's confident, or happy, or merely content by the smallest shift in the curve of his lips. For instance, the way his lower lip is sloping down right now means he's mulling something over. My favorite look is when he lifts the right side of his mouth just slightly, because when he does, it means that he's enjoying himself immensely.

"Stop looking at me like that, Sparky," he says.

I tilt my head. "Like what?" I ask.

"With your horny 'can't wait to find my soul mate' eyes," he says.

I grin and settle in for a good back and forth argument. I love this part of road trips. Long stretches with no coffee, bad. Arguments with Nick, good.

I flip down the visor and take a look at my eyes in the mirror. Hmm. Black mascara, sparkly taupe eyeshadow, and yup, sure enough, horn dog eyes. But, honest, I wasn't thinking about Matt Smith, I was thinking about that shower from the other day. I could use another shower. We've been driving for the past twelve hours and I'm tired and sore. I snap the visor back up and turn to Nick.

"Better?" I ask.

He looks over and I flutter my eyelashes at him and cross my eyes.

He laughs. "Screwball."

"Thanks for earlier," I say. I already said it, but... "You really went above and beyond."

"Forget about it."

I can't though. "I've been getting you in some crazy situations with my soul mate hunt."

He hums an assent. "Don't worry, I think it'll be smooth sailing from now on."

"You think?" I ask.

"How could it get worse?"

"An ax murderer?" I say, recalling his words from earlier.

He laughs. "It's not gonna happen. We've paid our dues."

I nod and settle back into my seat. Nick's lip tilts up and I can tell he's thinking about something he likes. His hands are stroking along the steering wheel and I can almost feel it like he's touching me.

I clear my throat. "So, I've been fantasizing about a new greeting card line." For some reason, I want him to be as excited about this idea as I am. I bounce up and down in my seat, squirming with the need to tell him more.

"Fantasizing, huh?"

"Yes," I say. Now that the dam's let loose I'm unable to stop. "That's what I do. I dream up ideas all the time. Anything can set me off, an overheard conversation, a picture, a moment. Once a baby threw up in his dad's hair and then the hair falls off and it turned out to be a toupee and that made me think about..." I trail off.

Nick has the goofiest smile on his face. "What?"

"I like your fantasies," he says.

I roll my eyes. "I'm not going to share all my fantasies."

"Uh huh," he says. "So that toupee made you come up with the 'hell toupee' card?"

"You saw it?" I ask. I clap my hands together and chortle. "Oh my gosh. Who'd you give it to? You buy my cards? Wait a minute..." I stop. "Are you my stalker? Do you have all my greeting cards in a scrapbook that you take out and palm through while listening to sappy songs?"

Nick clears his throat and then turns to me. "My mom sent me cards every month I was stationed in Afghanistan."

"Oh, right. Oh." I feel like a total jerk. Things just got weird. "Um. Well, anyway."

"Tell me about your idea," he says.

"Really?" I ask. My voice is high, so I clear my throat and try again. "Really?" That's better.

"Yeah, I want to hear it."

"Okay, so check this out..." I pull my drawing pad from the backseat and quickly sketch a scene. "There's this cat. He's this cranky loner cat who hates everybody and just wants to be left alone." I draw the outline of a cat with hooded eyes and dark fur. "And then there's this dog, and the dog loves everybody and everything and is—"

"Your spirit animal?"

"Nooo," I say. "The dog is in love with the cat."

Nick shakes his head and gives me that special Nick look that makes me squirm. I draw the dog. It's a big floppy-eared, big-eyed, happy puppy. I hold up the page to him with my cat and dog illustration. "See. And in each card they're having a different adventure and...you hate it."

"No. It's good," he says. He looks back at the road. "You should do it."

"Yeah?" I ask.

He stares straight ahead, even though I want him to look at me so I can see what he's thinking.

"Definitely," he says.

"Okay, I will." I sketch for a while, the ideas coming fast. Nick keeps peeking over and making sounds of approval. I'm giving the illustration my full attention and the miles fly by. Soon, we're past Denver, and Matt Smith Number Four isn't far.

"It's getting late, maybe we shouldn't go tonight?" I ask.

The sunset paints sherbet orange against the dusty purple mountains. I've never been this far west before and the rich colors and the high peaks that jut into the sky inspire me. But the encroaching night makes me question showing up on a stranger's mountain stoop. Maybe I'm starting to see Nick's point of view. We don't know this guy.

"Nah, we'll make it before eight. We can get a hotel after," Nick says.

"But like you said, he could be a psycho."

We've turned onto a dark mountain road. There are no

street lamps and no houses. Nick drives slowly over the pothole-ridden pavement and the car groans.

"She gonna make it?" I ask.

He sighs and pats the steering wheel. "It's alright, Shelly, she doesn't mean it."

I bite my lip to stop from smiling. I don't know why he insists that Shelly has feelings, the weirdo. I look out the window at the passing trees. I bet in the sunlight the forest is pretty, but right now my skin is crawling. The knots on the trees look like faces watching us pass and the limbs look like crooked fingers reaching down. A dark shadow swoops in front of us and I jump.

"Easy, it's just an owl," Nick says.

"Gah," I say.

We hit another pot hole and I bounce in my seat. I check the GPS, we're currently driving on a green splotch, as in, we've gone off any mapped roads.

"He'll be nice. He just likes nature. And solitude. And the dark," I say. "I mean the stars. Look at the beautiful stars."

You'd think I grew up in the city instead of a small town, but this kind of isolation is new to me. Even in the country outside Romeo, there are still neighbors. Is this guy my Matt? And if he is, why is he living a half-hour car ride from any other human being? Maybe he just needs the love of a good woman.

"You're not worried?" I ask. I try to penetrate the deep black of the woods. The only thing I can see clearly is the narrow bit of road illuminated in the gray line of the headlights.

"It's fine. I like the woods."

I shake my head. "This whole thing just took an eerie turn to slasher movie territory and you're not even concerned. Oh no...I'm not a virgin."

Nick swerves a bit and then jerks the car straight. "What the heck are you talking about?"

I gesture at the woods, then at him and me. "We're heading into some Halloween freak fest and I'm not a virgin. You're the unsuspecting jock driving us toward the slasher and I'm the impure girl that has to die because...because...I lost my virginity in the back of this. Freaking. Car."

I bury my head in my hands. "Can we come back in the morning?"

Nick pulls over and puts the car in park. He rests his hand on my shoulder. "Hey," he says. He hesitantly runs his hand up and down my arm. I let the rhythm of his stroking set in. After a minute I lift my head.

"Better?" he asks.

I nod. I'm past my freak out. "Sorry, that was silly."

He shrugs then gestures out the window. "Shelly can't make the driveway. We'll have to walk from here."

I look at the side of the road. Sure enough, there's a two track and a painted sign that says *Smith's Landing*.

"Looks nice enough," says Nick.

He turns off the engine and we step out into the night. It's brisk, and before closing the door I grab a cardigan. Then I remember something.

"Hang on," I say. This is the perfect time to make use of Vee's birthday gift. When else will I be deep in the woods and in need of survival gear? I pull from my suitcase the multitool and pop it in my bra. Now, I'm prepared.

Nick locks the doors and we head up the hill. My chunky heels aren't the best shoes for walking on a dirt road, but they're probably the best option of all the heels I brought. Hopefully the driveway isn't too long.

I stumble and Nick looks over. When my heel sinks into a rut and I stumble a second time, Nick moves closer and holds out his arm. I look at it, then slowly reach out and loop my arm through his. It feels, it feels...right. Like we should always be touching. Or that we should've never stopped. I move my free hand to the inside of his forearm. He's wearing a T-shirt and my fingertips run over his skin. I draw my hands down then up and sink into the warm, dark feel of him. He pulls in a sharp breath and I sway closer. His sharp exhale falls over my upturned face.

His skin glows in the moonlight and I catch a flicker in his eyes. The forest falls quiet and the sound of crickets and tree frogs dampens. If I kissed him, what would happen? Would it feel as good as it once did? Would it feel as good as this?

I stand on my tip toes and close my eyes.

14

Nick

MATT SMITH NUMBER FOUR...

DANG, SHE'S ABOUT TO KISS ME AND I DON'T WANT TO STOP HER. But she'll never forgive me if her supposed soul mate is at the top of the mountain and I take advantage of her at the bottom. I don't want to be the guy she walks away from.

"Come on, Sparky. Your soul mate's waiting." Which sounds lame, I admit, but these are extenuating circumstances.

Her eyes snap open and I watch as they go from hazy to irritated in a second flat. With that, she stiffens and pushes away from me. Then, she brushes at her dress and straightens her cardigan.

"Right. Exactly. Right," she says. Then she marches forward. I stay just close enough to catch her in case her heels sink into a mole hole or catch on an uneven track.

"Stop hovering," she says. "I'm fine. Temporary insanity inspired by...non-creepy woods."

I quirk a smile she can't see. She slaps at a mosquito that keeps buzzing around our heads. Then she stops and points at a wooden sign nailed to a tree.

"What's that?" she asks.

We walk closer and I shine my phone's flashlight on it. "Go away," I say. "Huh. Alright." I shrug and keep walking. Chloe stays at the sign a second longer, then runs after me.

"What? That sign doesn't bother you? Shouldn't we turn around?"

"Nah, it's fine. People in the country have those signs. It's standard protocol." In fact, I was planning on posting no trespassing signs on my land. I want to be left alone. That's why a lot of people move to the country, for peace and quiet.

We walk on a little more with nothing happening. "See. It's fine," I say.

After a bit, Chloe stops again and points at another tree. "What about that one?" she asks.

I shine my flashlight on it and read, "No trespassing."

"I think we should turn around," she says.

I shake my head. I'm invested in this now, we're more than halfway up the hill and I'm not turning around. It's not like we're in a war zone. "We don't have time. We have to leave for Nevada by six a.m."

I keep moving and Chloe scrambles after me.

"I'm just saying, don't you think it's kind of creepy?"

"No, I think it's normal. If you have property in the wilderness, you get signs. No trespassing. No hunting. It goes with the territory. It's fine."

"Fine," she says.

We keep walking. The night bugs get louder and I spot a few animal eyes reflecting in the moonlight. There are quite a few shed deer antlers along the trail. Finally, through the thick of the trees, I see a light shining. That has to be the house. It's maybe a quarter mile away.

An eerie screeching laugh echoes through the night followed by a shrill scream.

"What's that?" Chloe asks.

She moves closer to me but doesn't take my arm.

"Screech owl," I say. If I didn't know what one sounded like, it would scare the pants off me.

Chloe rubs her arms, then points at another sign, although I'd already seen it.

She reads it aloud. "Trespassers will be shot."

"It's fine," I say.

She shakes her head and folds her arms over her chest. "Nope. I'm not taking another step."

"Come on," I say. I move toward the house. "See, it's fine." I take another dozen steps. "See, completely and totally—"

I wrench back. Pain bursts.

Chloe screams.

I swat at the pain in my chest.

"Gol dermit…he shot me," I say. Then I lose control of my body and I crash to the ground. As my vision goes gray and hazy I spy another sign. It says, *Told You So.*

15

Nick

I'M DREAMING.

Chloe has me tied to a bed and I can't get free. She's dancing over me, her hair falling in soft curls brushing over my skin, and all I want to do is touch her. I beg her to untie me, but she won't. The need to touch her is burning through me. It's agony being tied down, but instead of freeing me she starts to undress. More than anything in the world, I want let free so I can touch her. But she stays just out of reach.

Untie me, I beg.

She laughs and takes a bite of chocolate cake. Her tongue swirls around the fork and I groan.

Untie me, please, I beg.

Wake up, she says.

Untie me.

"Dang it, Nick. Wake up," she says.

I jerk awake and flinch. "I'm awake," I say. My voice is scratchy and my throat is burning dry. I try to open my eyes and then I realize that they are open. We're in a pitch black room that smells like unwashed sheets and years of dust. I go to move and realize I can't.

"What the?" I tug and feel the bite of cold steel. Holy heck. I'm handcuffed.

"Chloe?"

"I'm here," she whispers.

"What happened?"

I listen for her in the dark. I hear her rustling on fabric nearby, I think she's only a few feet away. Her movement sends her soft familiar scent to me. I spread my hands and feel cold metal bars and fabric beneath them. I'm sitting on a carpeted floor and it feels like I'm cuffed to the footboard of a bed.

"Are you on a bed?" I ask.

"Yes. It's Matt Smith."

I swear. She was right. Or I was right back at the medieval dinner theatre. This Matt Smith is a psychopath.

"Did he...?" I ask, even though I'm terrified of the answer.

"No. I'm fine."

I try to feel around to figure out how I'm restrained. The key here is not to panic. Panic in a situation like this and it's over. Also, don't give up. The minute you start thinking you're dead, you are.

"Can you get loose?"

"No," she says. "I'm handcuffed to a metal bedframe. I've been trying for like an hour."

I feel around to see if I can find any weak spots. "I'm going to get us out of here. Hang tight."

"He thinks his ex-wife sent us. He didn't believe me when I told him the story about summer camp and soul mates." She pauses and then says, "He never went to summer camp."

"Well, that's an upside."

She's quiet while I work at the cuffs.

"He really hates his ex-wife," she says. "Did you know there are Happy Divorce Day cards?"

"That's too much," I say. I keep my voice light so she doesn't sense that the longer it takes me to get loose, the more worried I'm getting.

I work my hands around the contours of the footboard. The metal rail I'm cuffed to is about three inches around. I slide the cuff up and down the rail and determine that it's about two feet long. The thing is thick and solid, but maybe not unbreakable. I could kick it, or try to find a weak point. If nothing else, I could break a wrist to get out of the cuff. I need to hurry though. I don't know how much time we have.

"How long was I out?" I ask.

"A little over an hour. He shot you with a tranquilizer."

So that's why I'm not feeling any pain, just a pounding headache and a hellish thirst. I feel mildly reassured that I'm not going to bleed out before I can get Chloe out of here.

"Nick?"

"I'm here," I say. It's dark in this room. I can't see two feet in front of me. No windows. Nothing. I contort until my leg is lodged against the rail and then I press as hard as I can. The darn thing won't even bend.

"If we're gonna die—"

"We're not going to die," I say.

"But if we do. I forgive you...for the flagpoles."

I shake my head and then realize she can't see me. "I don't know what you're talking about."

She shifts on the bed. "The flagpoles. The day after we had sex," she says meaningfully.

"What?" I remember the day we had sex. It was both of our

first times and the best day of my young life. The day after, when she dropped me, was the worst.

"The flagpoles. You hung seven pairs of my panties on all the flagpoles around Romeo. The elementary school, the library, the post office, the high school, city hall, they all had my undies and a sign—Chloe Daniels is a bad lay."

"What?" I ask. "What the hell?"

I kick at the bed. It doesn't budge.

"You...wait. You don't know what I'm talking about?"

"No. No idea. I left town, remember? My dad had a heart attack in Albany. I left town and two hours later you phoned to say you never wanted to see me again."

"But you told me I wasn't worth the trouble," she says.

"I was eighteen. The girl I loved told me she hated me, that I was the scum of the earth and she never wanted to see my nasty face again. Meanwhile, my dad was in a hospital bed dying. What did you expect me to say?"

I kick at the footboard again. Hard. With about ten years of pent up frustration.

"Your dad was dying?" she asks.

"Didn't you hear that through the Romeo grapevine?" Usually there's no shortage of information.

"No. Nobody talked to me about you or your family after the flagpole fiasco. Everybody in town assumed you did it." Her voice is small in the dark.

I want out of these handcuffs so I can pull her into my arms. Ten years of misunderstanding, over what? Some insane prank that I never even knew about. I kick at the rail again. I think it's started to give way. There's a slight bend in the metal. If I can keep kicking at the weak spot it should snap. Then I'll be able to get us out of this nightmare.

"How would I have done it?" I ask. "How would I have seven pairs of your underwear? And why?"

I aim my hardest kick yet and the rail I'm cuffed to groans. The whole bed shudders. I feel the footboard with my hand. Yes, there's a crack there. A few more hits and I'll be free.

"You could've snuck into my room," she says, but her voice is full of doubt.

"Really?"

"Or maybe they weren't mine, but you went and bought some that looked exactly like mine."

"Are you kidding me?" I grab the metal and try again to pry it loose.

"But who else would've done it?"

"I don't know, but *why* would I?"

Silence. Then, "I've been such an idiot," she says. Her voice is thick. "I lost you. And it's because I'm a complete and utter idiot."

I close my eyes at the sharp pain in her voice. "You're not," I say.

"I am. It's my fault. And now we're going to..."

There's pressure in my chest so I kick out at the rail again. It bends and then cracks. Only half the metal is connected, and it looks hollow inside. Hallelujah for cheap manufacturing. One more kick and we'll be free.

"Chloe. It's alright. You didn't lose me. I'm right here," I say. "Don't cry. It's okay, Sparky. It's okay. Really. I never stopped—"

I'm cut off, and maybe saved from making a really stupid confession.

"I did it," Chloe says. "I'm free, the multitool freaking worked," I hear Chloe jump off the bed and rush toward me. She did it. She freed herself, she's free. "Vee was right. We're going to be okay."

She reaches me and—

Suddenly, the door crashes open. Light shines in and I squint my eyes against the sharp glare. There's a huge grizzly bear-sized man in the doorway. He's bearded, flannelled, and holding a gleaming metal ax.

Chloe screams.

"Ready to die, mother effers?"

16

Chloe

I SCREAM. AND SCREAM. AND SCREAM.

Until I realize that the big, crazy man with the ax is laughing hysterically. And not in the maniac ax murderer kind of way, but in the "I just played the best practical joke of my life" way.

"Phoned the ex-wife," he says in a booming voice. "She ain't got a clue who you are. Figure your crazy soul mate story's true. Anywho..." He hefts the ax in his hand. "Y'all want some chow? I got fatback on the griddle."

In the next few minutes I take on an all new appreciation for Nick. His wrists are bloody and starting to bruise and he looks like he could chew through metal he's so mad, but he crams it all back inside and plays along with the insane mountain man.

We refuse the late night snack of fatback and extricate ourselves from small talk and niceties as quickly as possible.

The whole while I peek at Nick and wonder exactly what he was about to say. I never really stopped...what?

We hike back down the hill, and I gingerly step over the uneven two track. When we're out of sight of the house, Nick grabs my hand and then we run as fast as we can. He steadies me when I trip over a stump and then we start running again. When we make it to Shelly, I'm out of breath and all cut up from the brambles and prickers.

Nick hugs Shelly's hood, and I'm so happy to see her that I almost do too. But then Nick turns to me and after I see the look on his face, I take a step back.

"Never again, Sparky," he says. "I'm never coming back to Colorado. The insane, lunatic, deranged love children of Davy Crockett and Wolverine."

Huh.

"He did have signs," I say. Because...signs.

Nick's eyes go all crazy and the emotion that he crammed inside earlier comes rushing out. He leaps at me. "I'll show you a sign," he says. His eyes are wild.

I yelp and run around the car. Soon he's chasing me one way then another, with Shelly as the buffer between us.

"I'll give you a sign, Chloe Daniels, so help me God."

He lunges at me and nearly grabs me. At the last minute I jump on the hood and slide across it. I can barely breathe I'm laughing so hard. Then, as I slide, my dress flips up and I flash Nick my thong.

He stops, stunned. Then, his eyes flood with a fiery *need*. I scramble off the hood. My heart pounds. He stalks around the car and I back away until my legs hit the door. Nick leans forward and cages me against it. He rests his arms on either side of me and leans in until I'm completely surrounded by his heat. There's a flicker low in my belly, and I resist the urge to push myself against him. I lick my lips and he watches the movement like he's about to pounce.

"Don't...don't pay attention to the full moon," I say, referring to my flashing him. "It makes people do crazy things."

He lifts a lock of my hair and rubs it between his fingers. "Crazy's right," he says.

Why is my heart pounding harder now than it was when I was handcuffed to a maniac's bed?

Nick tugs a bit on my hair and I let out a low moan. Then he picks me up and puts me on Shelly's hood. He pulls me against him and gently wraps my legs around him. I can feel how hard he is, his length presses against me. He watches my face and takes in my expression.

"What are you doing?" I whisper.

"Looking for a sign," he says. Then he pulls me harder against him. I grab his shoulders and reflexively run myself down his length. He's bigger than I remember, and thicker. My pulse picks up.

He moans and then brings his lips a millimeter from mine.

"I've been wanting to test something," he says.

"What?" I can't keep up. I don't know where this is headed.

He takes the back of my neck and shoves his lips over mine. I cry out and open my mouth to him and he plunges in.

Yes.

I claw my fingers into his shoulders and scramble up against him, wanting to get closer, wanting more. I wrap my legs tighter and make a desperate noise in my throat. I need him. He picks me up and backs me against the window. He runs his length against me and I start to ride him. The pressure of his length against me is heaven and I never want to stop riding him. My mouth is still open to him, my tongue tangling with his.

This isn't a sweet kiss. Or a hesitant kiss. Heck no. I'm clawing at him, trying to climb in deeper, harder, faster. I yank on his hair. I want more. It's not enough. I run myself up and down him and feel the growing, mindless need. It's consuming me. I nip at his mouth and he bucks against me. He grabs my hair and holds me in place so his mouth can have control over mine. He's just as demanding as me. More. I ride on his length. He's trapped in his jeans, and suddenly, I want him free. I want his pants off and my dress flipped up and me bent over the hood and...

A gunshot cracks through the night.

I startle back and Nick almost drops me.

"What the—?" he says.

"Jeez," I say.

It feels like a glass of ice water was just thrown over me. I'm startled and cold without Nick around me. And I'm breathing like I just ran the New York City marathon. I don't know about mine, but his eyes are nearly pitch black and full of hunger and need. He gently sets me down on the hood and turns away.

I smooth my dress and stand on wobbly legs.

He takes a second to collect himself. When he turns back he looks almost normal again.

"We better get out of here," he says.

I nod. What the heck just happened and how in the world do I go forward from here?

We climb into the car and he drives down the pothole-strewn road. Finally, after an incredibly long and awkward silence, I manage to pull my thoughts together enough to say..."So, what the heck was that?"

Nick scowls. "That, Sparky, was a sign."

"Like..."

"Like, go away, no trespassing."

I rub my hands over my arms and don't ask whether the no trespassing is for him or for my Matt Smith. I look down at my legs, they're scratched up and a little bloody. I feel dirty and gross.

"I need a shower."

"Dang, I'm glad to be alive," he says. He runs a hand over the steering wheel and lovingly strokes the dashboard. "Shelly, my love, I thought for a second I'd never see you again."

I smile. What a weirdo.

Then I remember what I'd been wondering about after our "near death" experience and all that we'd said.

"Nick, back there you said something about never stopping?"

He shakes his head hard. His mouth sets in a firm line, the one that says he's decided to be stubborn and take his secrets to the grave. I melt a little. His hair is mussed, he's bloody, bruised, and clearly exhausted. He should look awful, but to me he looks...

"Leave it alone, Sparky," he says.

"But..."

"It's in the past."

"But what about that kiss?" I ask.

"It's in the past, too. You're after your Matt, and we're behind schedule," he says more firmly.

I sigh. "Fine. But can we at least get a shower and some sleep before heading to Vegas?"

The answer is yes.

We each get our own hotel room, and I don't know about him, but I take a thirty-second shower and collapse into sleep. I dream that Nick changes his name to Matt and then chains me to a bed and licks my naked body. The whole time he growls, "Who's eating the love sugar now?"

17

Nick

Two days left...

It's a long trek to Vegas, and the closer I get the more I want to turn around. There are only two potentials left, and Chloe is betting everything that one of these guys is her true love. Let me tell you why that's really starting to piss me off. Number one, she shouldn't let some mumbo jumbo dictate her future. Number two, the more I see of her, the more I want to keep seeing her. For the rest of my life.

That's it.

That's the awful truth that makes this drive to Vegas feel like a walk to the gallows. I can finally admit that I want Chloe. But she wants someone else, and instead of making her mine, I'm taking her to another man.

I'm in a piss poor mood today, and seeing the flashy sings of Vegas isn't helping.

"What's wrong?" asks Chloe. "You've been grinding your teeth since we crossed the state line." That was an hour ago. We've been on the road for nearly twelve hours today, since six a.m. mountain time.

She's right, I have been tense. She was upset when she came out of her room this morning, but after sketching for a few hours she relaxed. But me, the closer we get to Vegas, the more my blood pressure goes up.

"I don't like gambling," I say.

She stares at my profile when I don't say anything more. "Because of your dad," she says.

I look over to see if she's judging me, or if she's feeling pity, but neither's there. She's just listening. I let go of some of the tension.

"I hate casinos, so a city full of them isn't my favorite place."

When we were together I told her some about my dad, not everything, but even then I didn't know the full extent of the problem.

"I saw him once, at the return counter in Walmart. He had a bag full of frozen vegetables and canned food. My mom had been on me to stop eating us out of house and home for months. We barely had enough money to eat as it was. I didn't eat much, I skipped meals to help out. I couldn't figure it out." I look over at her.

"He was returning your food for money?"

I nod. "Anything he could get his hands on."

"No wonder you loved coming over for dinner. I just thought you liked my mom's cooking. I didn't realize you were—"

"Don't," I say. "I wasn't."

"So what did you do?"

"I watched the cashier hand him thirty-two dollars and seventeen cents, then I followed him to the casino where he lost it in one play."

That's why I hate casinos. "He was at a casino outside of Albany when he had a heart attack. He finally won big, five thousand dollars. It was enough to cover the funeral. After that, we realized he'd double mortgaged the house and taken on more debt than my mom could ever repay."

I think back to the hell of that week. The hungry years before that week were nothing. My dad, in his own way, shielded us from realizing the extent of his problem. I didn't know whether to thank him or hate him for it. Ten years later, I realize he was just a human, making human mistakes.

"So you went into the military?" Chloe asks.

I nod. "I was eighteen. The only way I could see digging my mom and sisters out of it was by joining the military."

"Nick," she says. And the way she says my name makes me turn to her, there are tears at the corners of her eyes. She's looking at me like I'm some kind of hero.

"Quit looking at me like that," I say.

She turns away and swipes at her eyes.

I need a change of topic. So, I bring up what's been gnawing at me since yesterday. "I think I figured out your flagpole situation," I say.

She jerks back to me. "What?"

"I think I know who did it." It's obvious now that I've had a chance to think about it.

"Who?"

"Ron."

She shakes her head. "Come on. As much as I'd like to pin all the world's ills on him, I'm not going to make Ron the scapegoat. Yeah, we all know he's a jerk, but why would seventeen-year-old Ron steal my underwear? Honestly, you have no idea how much this destroyed my teenage years. The older ladies in town gave me the evil eye, I lost my babysitting clients, I became a pariah at school. It took years to get past it. And yet, Ron never spoke to me until I was in my twenties. He had no motive."

"Remember fifth grade, when Zoe Torres started wearing real bras?"

"Yes," she says. "I was jealous."

"Ron stole them and hung them in the boys' locker room."

"What?" She looks at me disbelievingly. "No."

"Then, in ninth grade, he stole Jan Zhang's bikini—"

"The head cheerleader Jan Zhang?"

"That's right. And he brought it out for good luck rubs before football games. And then in eleventh grade he stole Mrs. Hightower's—"

"The biology teacher?"

"That's right."

"Stop. I don't want to know."

"Then you don't want to hear about Miss Stunk's Spanx?"

"No, stop. Ack. I feel dirty." She shivers and then wipes her hands off on her legs.

I raise an eyebrow. "So...Ron?"

She takes out her phone and types out a quick text. Thirty seconds later a ping sounds, then another.

"What's up?"

"I'm texting Vee. She's texting Zoe and Jan."

I shake my head. "Don't believe me?"

"I'm just getting confirmation."

Another ping sounds. "Okay. Fine. They both confirmed it... Vee says Ron admitted years ago that he did it. Zoe thought I knew."

"Yeah," I say. My shoulders relax. It was a hunch, but I'm not surprised. "I guess that means my good name's cleared."

"I'm sorry." She sighs and drops her chin to her chest. "Sometimes I wish I could go back in time and tell myself not to make the mistakes that I did."

I reach over and chuck her under her chin. She looks up at me in surprise.

"Then you wouldn't be you," I say. "And where's the fun in that?"

The corner of her lip lifts into a small kissable smile and she nods. "Huh. I guess so. Plus, now I can blame all the ills in the world on Ron."

"That's the spirit," I say.

"I really am sorry," she says.

"Don't worry about it. Like I said, it's in the past. You've got your Matt Smith to find." This comes out more curt than I'd intended.

She sends me a sharp look. But there's no more time for talk. We've made it to our next stop.

I pull into the address I have for Matt Smith Number Five. It's a comic shop in an old 1990s-style strip mall. There's a long squat row of connected shops with small windows, cracked sidewalks, and an empty parking lot. The comic shop is called Rodney's Comics.

We walk through the dry heat of Vegas into the shop. The bells on the door jingle and the smell of freshly printed comic books and the blast of ice-cold air conditioning hits us.

There's nobody in the shop except for a big guy behind the counter. He has stick-straight black hair and the build of a pro wrestler. Chloe walks up to him and smiles.

"Hey there. I'm looking for Matt Smith," she says.

I walk up next to her and put my fists in my pockets. What do you know? She's getting better at approaching the topic of soul mates with complete strangers.

The big guy leans over the desk and looks at the both of us

from the tops of our heads to the tips of our shoes. I haven't had such a thorough looking over since military inspection.

"What? Are you friends of Matt's from FurCon?" he asks.

I look at Chloe. I don't think she knows what he's talking about either.

"Um...that's...because...what?" she asks.

The guy chuckles and I think it's at our expense. "Matt's at FurCon."

Chloe perks up. She smiles and nods, "Yes. I mean, absolutely. We want to go to vercom."

"FurCon," I say.

She nods quickly, "Vercon."

The big guy looks at me and slowly shakes his head. His long hair falls over his left eye and he swipes it aside. "You have no idea, do you?"

I hold up my hands. "I got nothing."

He puts on a long-suffering sage look, then swings up the counter divider and steps out. He waves his hand. "Follow."

He has a limp and swings his right leg to the side as he walks. We walk behind him as he throws comments over his shoulder every few steps. "Matt's a furry," he says.

"Okay?" says Chloe.

"A coyote. There's all kinds of animals, but Matt feels most comfortable as a coyote."

"He's a coyote?" I ask, trying for clarification.

The guy stops and sends me a look like I'm a few crayons short of a box. "He's a furry. They have meetings all over the U.S. He'll be at this con for the next three days."

"But we need to see him," says Chloe.

The guy turns and continues walking toward the back of the store. It's dim and musty. A few of the fluorescent lightbulbs are burned out. There are rows of shelves, deep with comic books covered in plastic sheets, models, and gaming stuff. The store is long and narrow and jam packed with merchandise. We come to a stop at the end of a narrow aisle.

Chloe probably can't see around him, but I can.

"The only way you'll see him," says the big guy, "is as a furry."

He steps aside.

Chloe gasps and then steps back. "Oh no," she says.

"What?" I ask.

"Puppets. I hate puppets."

The big guy rolls his eyes. "Those aren't puppets."

"I have to wear one of those to see Matt?" she asks.

I'm getting concerned, she looks like she's about to be sick.

"Or wait three days until he comes back to work," says the guy. "Your choice. They're two hundred a pop."

Is this guy serious?

There's no way to tell. Chloe looks at me, gauging my reaction. Will I help her or won't I? Will I do this or not? I step forward and grab the only fuzzy animal costume that looks big enough to fit me.

"I've always felt most comfortable as…" I hold up the suit.

The big guy snorts.

Chloe starts to laugh and then that determined light fills her eyes.

She's back in the game.

18

Chloe

MATT SMITH NUMBER FIVE...

I'M TRUSSED UP IN A FULL-BODY HOT PINK PANDA COSTUME. IT smells like Cheetos and jockstrap. Even though the head is open, it's a hood sort of thing, I can still smell the old scratchy fur with every breath I take.

It's hotter than a sauna in this panda, and it's itchy. Unfortunately, my hands are paws and it's impossible to scratch myself. But I least I look cute. Right? Who wouldn't look adorable as a pink panda bear with a fuzzy white belly and soft fur?

"This is worse than the proctologist," says Nick.

I look over at him and grin. "You look great."

He narrows his eyes.

"I'm dressed as a cock," he says.

"It's a rooster."

It's fuzzy white with a red comb, a tail, and yellow legs like big bird. He scowls at me from between a big yellow beak.

"Don't worry. You're the cutest cock I've ever seen," I say.

He raises his eyebrows. "Let's get this over with."

I'm still readjusting, trying to reconcile the fact that everything I've believed of Nick for the past ten years was wrong. He never set out to hurt me, he wasn't responsible for the flagpoles, he didn't know about the wedding, he's always been...good.

That's almost scarier though than him being a jerk, because then, how do I stop myself from wanting him? Because I do. Except, I called Aunt Erma earlier, and she reassured me that I was on the right track with my hunt. So. Forward.

We stride into the hotel ballroom where the Vegas furries are meeting. No one really notices as we come in. Not that I blame them. What's two more fuzzy people in a crowd of a hundred? The ballroom is the usual boring hotel bland. Fluorescent lighting, beige wallpaper, dark red carpet. What makes this room different than the usual is the pile in the center of the room of about thirty people in animal costumes laying on top of each other. The guy at the comic shop mentioned this—it's called a fur pile.

"Which one of these guys do you think is Number Five?" asks Nick. He surveys the room.

I look over the big group. I have no clue.

A man and a woman in brown bear costumes nuzzle on a low couch nearby. Another group stands near a refreshments table.

"Let's go ask," I say.

Nick studies me. "You sure?"

Is this like when he asked me in the prison? I study his face, but he doesn't seem to have any deeper meaning to his words.

"Can't be worse than Colorado," I say. At least everyone here seems friendly.

We walk across the room to where a small group of furries stand by a table piled with carrot sticks, ranch dip, pita bread and hummus. There are a few two liters of Coke.

The group is in a heated discussion about the future of furry conventions.

I move in a little closer and wave a pink paw. "Hi there. I'm Chloe."

A freckled man with glasses wearing a raccoon suit stops talking. They all turn to stare.

"You're new," says the raccoon man. He looks me up and down then says, "Nice."

Nick steps next to me and puts his hand on my arm.

"Um. I'm looking for Matt Smith. Do you know if he's here?"

"He was in the pile," says a girl dressed as a fox, "but he went for a smoke." She shrugs then winks at Nick. "You want to go in with me?"

"That's alright," he says. His face turns a shade darker.

"Too bad," she says, "I like your cock-stume."

He chokes a little and coughs. I pat his back. Music starts up from the DJ in the corner, it's a sort of techno dance mix.

"The dancing is starting. Wanna dance?" the fox asks.

I elbow Nick in the ribs. I don't think he feels it because his costume is thickly padded around the middle. He's staring at foxy girl like he's never seen anything like her in his life. I elbow him again.

He snaps out of it. "Um, no. That's alright."

"You sure? Foxes love to eat...chickens," she says.

"No means no," I snap. I am not jealous of the foxy girl. Not at all.

I pull Nick away from the group and back toward the door.

"Let's just wait here until he comes back," I say. But Nick shakes his head.

"We have to blend," he says. He nods at the crowd. We're starting to attract attention. Not because we're dressed as a pink panda and a rooster, but because we're standing at the entry like two creepy lurkers. Half of the people are still in the fur pile, but the other half are dancing. I don't want to go in the pile...so.

"Let's dance."

I grab Nick's hand and lead him to the center of the room. We start to bounce to the music and jump up and down to the techno beat. Soon, we get into it and I forget that I'm afraid of fuzzy puppet-like creatures and start to get into it.

"You're pretty good," says Nick. "Not a bad dancer for a panda."

I punch him in the arm. "You're not too bad yourself."

He smiles at my compliment and I bump my hips against him. After a few minutes my heart's pounding and I'm sweating buckets. My hair is plastered to my head and sweat trickles between my breasts. I'm relieved when the song ends and a slow acoustic melody starts to play. It's a slow dance. I glance around the room. Furries are pairing off into couples and swaying back and forth to the music.

Nick holds out his hands with a questioning look on his face.

"Okay," I say.

It's funny, I remember the same look on his face back in high school when he first asked me out. It said, please don't hurt me. Boys are more vulnerable than girls know.

I step toward him and put my paws on his shoulders. He wraps his hands around my waist. It feels a little like a junior high dance when we had to keep our bodies three feet apart. Except this time, instead of the rules keeping us apart, it's our padded bellies. He pulls me closer, until our fur is pressed tight together. A hot pulse rolls through me and I close my eyes. We rock back and forth to the song, while a delicious warmth sings through my veins. It's kind of strange dancing with Nick as a big, fuzzy animal rather than as himself. It's like there's not all the history and the humanness to keep us apart. I lean in and rest my head against his chest. His hands close over my back and linger at the base of my spine. We sway to the music, and suddenly, I don't want this moment to ever end. I can hear his heart pounding through my hood. His hands dip a half inch lower and I move closer. I rub the velvety fur of his costume and relax into him even more.

He tilts his head and runs his lips across my forehead. "Chloe," he says.

"Yes?" My eyes flutter open and I look up at him.

"Do you think..."

My heart beat picks up. "Yes?"

He leans down and runs his lips over mine. He tastes of salt and fresh air and desire. I close my eyes and revel in the feel of him. The cool taste of his lips and the sharp puff of his exhale. The warmth of him as he opens his mouth and pulls on my bottom lip.

I revel in it. But then, I remember, I'm not a pink panda, I'm a human, looking for my soul mate. And even if thinking of being with Nick sends an ache through me...he's not mine.

Finally, the music stops and Nick pulls away.

"Do you think..." he says again, "that you might..."

I have to stop him before he asks the question. I know where he's going and I can't.

"I can't," I say. "I'm sorry."

He pulls his hand away from me and steps back. "Right. I forgot." His lips twist into a deep scowl and he wipes the back of his mouth with his hand.

I look down at the floor and blink back tears. Nick and I wouldn't work. He's not my soul mate, my Aunt Erma confirmed it just this morning. And that's the only thing I need to know to make this decision. I look back up at him, wiping my face of all expression. "I'm looking for my soul mate, not..." I pause.

He studies my face, then his expression becomes hard. "Someone like me."

"No." I shake my head. "I don't know. You're not my soul mate."

But whereas before I was ecstatic that he wasn't, now it hurts that he's not. I want him to be. I want him so much. But I'm too scared to say that out loud.

"I'm sorry," I say instead.

"You want something to drink?" He nods toward the table.

He's letting me off the hook. We walk over to the table and I take a cup. The raccoon guy walks over. "Hey, your coyote is in the fur pile," he says.

I turn and look. Sure enough, a blonde guy dressed as a coyote is on the edge of the pile.

"Alright. Thanks." Nick motions toward the pile. "Let's do this."

We stride over to the edge of the furries. When we get there I have to go down on all fours to get close to Matt. He's on top of a polar bear and under a rabbit.

"Matt Smith?" I ask.

His eyes are closed and he rubs his hands over the polar bear's fur. When I say his name his eyes open. When he sees my costume his face lights up.

"I love bears," he says.

"I'm Chloe."

The girl in the bunny costume reaches out and runs her hand down my arm. I scoot back a bit.

"Hey there, Chloe bear," he says. "There's plenty of room. Come on in."

"Did you go to summer camp in New York?" I ask.

Matt's distracted by the rabbit fur rubbing over his face. He strokes his fingers through the fabric and tugs on her long ears.

"Matt? Did you? Because I really need to know."

The polar bear guy growls and rolls over to face me. "Hey, Miss Panda. I'm his bear. I don't share with other bears."

I inch back, balance on my knees and hold up my paws. "No. It's cool, I just..." I look at Matt. His face is buried in the bunny's furry backside. I move back onto my hands and crawl closer to Matt. "Excuse me. Can I talk to you outside for a second?"

His head cocks to the side, then he looks me up and down. "Yeah?"

I nod. "Yeah."

"Awesome."

The polar bear growls again.

"Mellow, Stan. I'll be back in fifteen," Matt says.

Nick pulls me up from the floor.

"We can go out the door there," says Matt, pointing at an exit on the far wall. "I need a cigarette."

We leave the room and step out into the early evening. Even though it's Vegas and a dry ninety degrees, the fresh air still feels wonderful. Matt unzips his suit and pulls out a pack of Marlboros and a lighter. "Want one?"

"No, thanks."

He holds the pack out to Nick.

"Nah."

We're behind the hotel in the parking lot. Nick's car is parked in the front row less than twenty feet away. Matt pulls in a long, long draw. He looks across the lot at Shelly.

"Now that's a nice ride," he says. "Used to take joyrides in a lady like her."

I let him take another long draw as we all admire Shelly. She's a little dusty from the trip, but still, I admit, she looks good. Nick was right, she hasn't let us down. Not once.

I ask my question again. I'm antsy and itchy and Nick's kisses are making me uncomfortable and I just want to get this trip over with so the confusion can stop.

"Did you go to summer camp in New York?"

Matt turns to me. His coyote costume gives him a trickster sort of vibe. He even has a wily glint in his eyes. "If I say yes, will you skritch with me?"

"Um." I don't know what skritch means, but I'm not sure I'll like it. "No," I say.

"Then no. I didn't."

I frown. "If I say yes, does that mean you did go to summer camp in New York?"

"I really like that car," Matt says.

Nick steps forward. "She's mine," he says. He says it in such a menacing way that at first I think he's talking about me. But neither of them are looking my way.

"Ohhh man. That's awesome. How's she ride?"

"Responsive. Smooth and tight."

"Yesss," says Matt.

I shake my head to clear it. They're talking about Shelly. The car. Jeez.

"Excuse me," I say. "I really need to know if you've ever been to summer camp in New York."

Matt shrugs and takes another puff of his cigarette. "Don't remember."

I sag against the brick wall of the hotel and close my eyes. Why? Why me?

Nick growls. "How about I tell your polar bear friend that

you skritched with four other bears out here unless you give us an answer," he says.

I push myself off the wall. Matt winces and throws down his cigarette. He steps on the still burning end with his paw.

"Did you?" I ask.

I can feel Nick watching me intently, but I keep my eyes on Matt. Finally, he shakes his head.

"No. Never did," he says.

My shoulders sag.

I don't want to look at Nick and see the expression on his face. I can't.

"Okay, thanks," I say.

Matt shrugs and slinks away.

I lean back against the brick wall and close my eyes. I'm...relieved.

When I open my eyes again, Nick stares down at me and he looks furious.

19

Nick

"WHY?" I ASK.

I clench my fists. I thought I could get through this without confronting her again, but I can't let it go, and I don't know how much more I can take. A guy with a cat fetish, a felon, a proctologist and a guy in a coyote costume...what do these guys have that I don't except a certain name?

"Why what?" Chloe asks. She swallows and I watch her throat bob. She should look awful dressed up as a panda, but instead she looks cute as hell and it only makes me want her more.

"Why are you doing this?" I gesture around us, at the costumes, the hotel, at the world.

"I already told you why," she says. She crosses her arms.

I pace in the space in front of her. "No. I don't buy it. None of what you said makes sense."

"I'm not talking about it," she says. She starts to walk away, farther from the door. I follow her, drawn to her. I have to figure this out. It's not just blind romanticism that's driving this.

"None of what you said would make you chase a stranger across the country. You've been willing to fall in love with a prisoner, a psycho, a stranger in a coyote costume. It's insane."

"It's not," she says. She lifts her chin in the air and glares. "It's not."

"Bull." I run a hand down my face. "It is. How can you be so smart but so stupid?"

"I'm not. My aunt told me—"

"It's not real. None of it's real."

She backs up and her chin shakes. I've hit a sore spot, but I can't stop. "You're deluded. You keep flitting around, all sunshine and sparkles, chipper and upbeat, thinking some messed up stranger is going to be your perfect fit."

"He will be," she says. Her eyes have a desperate look.

"He won't."

"There's one more," she says. "And it's him. My aunt said I'd find him on this trip. Tomorrow, I'll find him and I'll prove you wrong."

The thought terrifies me. I hadn't realized how much until this moment. Her words hit me like a fist. I want to roar. Instead I say, "It won't be him. Admit it."

"No," she says.

"Admit it. Soul mates aren't real."

A tear falls from her eyes and she swipes at it with a pink paw. "I won't," she says. "I'll never admit it."

I've backed her to a wall again. I'm standing over her, and all I want to do is kiss her and punish her until she admits that she's wrong.

"But you want to," I say.

She shakes her head to deny it.

"Throw out this soul mate garbage and make your own choice."

"No." Her face is pale but her eyes are determined. She won't, I see it now.

"Why?" I put my hands on the wall over her shoulders and lean into her. "Why?" I ask against her lips.

Another tear forms and her lips twist.

"Why, Chloe?"

"Because."

"Because, why?"

She pushes at me, but I won't let her out.

"Why?"

"Because."

"That's not good enough."

I've pushed her too far. A small sob escapes her. "Because," she cries, "if I try and it doesn't work, I'll break. I'll break, Nick."

She holds back another sob. I reach out and wipe away the tears on her face.

"I don't understand," I say.

She closes her eyes and drops her head.

"Help me understand. Please."

I reach out to wipe her tears. Then the roar of an engine cuts through the night. I stop, and spin around. I know that sound.

It's Shelly.

She tears out of her parking spot in reverse. My stomach drops. What the hell? Then she whips into drive and her tires spin on the asphalt, kicking up dirt and smoke.

"It's Matt," cries Chloe.

It is. He's taking her.

Shelly's wheels squeal shrilly and then she revs into drive.

I yell an expletive and sprint after her. I hear Chloe behind me. I can see a coyote head in the driver's seat. He's at the edge of the parking lot, waiting to turn onto the street.

"Stop," I yell. "Get out of my car."

I'm thirty feet away from her. I yell again. If he hurts her, if he wrecks her, or puts a single scratch on her, I swear to God. "Stop!"

I pump my arms and run faster. Matt looks back, and he must see me because he throws back his head and howls. Then he guns the engine and swerves into traffic.

Shelly fishtails and sends up rocks and dirt behind her. Cars honk and swerve around her. She barely avoids getting T-boned. I swear, I nearly have a heart attack. I can catch him, I have to catch him. There's stopped traffic ahead and a red light. I'll yank open the door and pull him out and...

He runs the red light. And the next. I run faster, sprint harder.

Shelly swerves around another car.

"Nick," I hear Chloe yelling behind me. But I can't stop.

There's another red light, this one has a cross walk. There are kids in the crosswalk. But I'm too far. I can't stop it and I can't stop Shelly and I can't save her and I can't...

Matt hits the brakes, Shelly swerves. He yanks her wheel and she spins in a circle. My heart stops. The kids...no, Shelly misses them. She hits the curb, ricochets, hits a dividing wall, then...

I've stopped running. It's all in slow motion.

Matt has jumped out of her door and is running down the street. A semi blares its horn, and then I watch, completely helpless to do anything as Shelly is swiped by the edge of the truck. She flips end over end. Each hit, I feel, like it's me flipping over. Once, twice, another. Then she comes to a stop. I start running again, before her final landing.

She's a car. Yes. I know she's just a car. But she's mine, she's my friend, and sometimes she was my only friend. The nights I thought I wasn't going to make it, when I wanted everything to just end, she pulled me through. And now, this is how I repay her. I let her get taken and I let her get hurt, and...

I run for her, mindless of the traffic around me, the horns and the cars and the shouts. I'm almost to her. I can fix her. I can fix her, it'll be okay. Her front is twisted, her windows are broken, her backend is crushed, but I can fix her. I can help her. Please.

Then, the fuel tank, a spark, something, I don't know. She catches fire. One minute, I'm almost to her, the next, I'm thrown back as she bursts into flames.

20

Nick

HOURS LATER, CHLOE AND I SIT ON THE CURB AND STARE AT THE charred area where Shelly burned. We gave a police statement and our information. There's nothing else to be done.

"He stole Shelly," says Chloe in a numb voice.

I nod. A heavy weight settles in my stomach. She's gone. I stare at the black scorch mark, the broken glass, and the bits of metal on the road. Shelly's been with me for such a long time that I never imagined her not being there. I keep expecting this to have been a weird hallucination and for her to still be in her parking spot back at the hotel.

"All our clothes, our money, our suitcases, it's all gone," Chloe says.

We're sitting on the curb in a rooster costume and a panda costume, with no clothing, no money and no phone. And no Shelly.

"But...we only have two days. I have to get to Matt Number

Six."

Slowly, I turn to stare at her. I just lost a piece of myself and all she cares about is that she doesn't have a ride to Matt Number Six. I clench my jaw and let out a long, slow breath.

"We weren't done," I say.

"What?"

"We didn't finish our conversation. Tell me why we have to get to him? Why can't we go home? Why can't you let this go? Choose someone on your own? Don't give me any bull crap about breaking. Tell me the truth."

She shakes her head and scoots farther away on the curb.

"Tell me," I growl. I'm too raw, I can't take evasion or misunderstandings anymore.

She flinches at my tone and her face drains of color. Then, she looks away and wraps her arms around herself. I see it then, she's hurting too.

"Are you okay?"

She drops her head to her knees, then after a long minute she looks up and starts to talk.

"I chose before," she says.

I nod. "Ron."

"I followed my heart, and I followed it wrong."

I start to respond, but she holds up her hand. "I can't be cynical like you, because if I gave in to that, I'd just lay down and give up forever. This 'deluded' hope is the only thing that keeps me going. That somewhere there's someone who is good and kind and who will love me forever and never, ever hurt me."

At the way she spits out the word "hurt," my heart twists in my chest.

"I chose a dozen times and each time I chose wrong. I'm done with choosing."

What I see in her face breaks my heart.

"So, here it is. I'm going to keep looking for him. And keep looking. It wasn't Ron. It wasn't the rest of them." She looks at me and lowers her voice to a whisper, "And it's not you, Nick. It's not you."

And that is what a nail in a coffin feels like. I know, because it just got pounded into my heart.

"I didn't know about the flagpole, or the wedding, I—"

"You left. You left me, and you never came back. You never even tried to explain, Nick. You just left." She stares down at her knees, then closes her eyes.

I did. I left her. I let her down, and really, I let us both down. I don't have any excuse, I could've called her, tried to set things right, but instead I got angry and cynical.

Right now, I want to go give Ron another round for hurting Chloe, and the rest of the guys in her past too. But, hey, I'm one of them...so.

She lowers her head and tries to hold back her tears. Her body shakes but she doesn't make a sound. She cries silent, quiet, aching tears. Dry tears that no one can see, so they don't know how much pain is inside.

"Chloe," I say. I hold out my hand to her, palm up, and wait. I let it hang between us. For thirty seconds, forty, a minute. Until finally, she reaches out and sets her hand in mine. Then she leans in and I hold her.

We sit on the curb and watch the cars go by. Sometimes, a car honks, or people shout. After all, we're two fuzzy animals on the side of the road. But mostly, we take in the quiet of falling night. I wait, thinking maybe a miracle will happen and Shelly will come back. I wait, thinking maybe Chloe will speak, but she doesn't. I run a thumb over her hand and hold her.

Finally, Chloe shifts away from me and clears her throat. "I forgave Ron. A long time ago. That was almost too easy," she says.

I squeeze her hand but don't interrupt.

She continues, "The one thing I've never been able to do is forgive myself." Her mouth turns down and a tear falls. "People think, why would someone who was hurt have to forgive herself? They don't understand. It's for everything. For being there. For staying. For trusting. For loving. For letting it happen. For not knowing it was going to happen. For being...what?...a person who attracted it. Like, what did I do to make this happen? What did I do? And then, I hate myself. I hate myself for being there, for seeing myself being hurt and not being able to stop it. Because shouldn't I have been able to stop it? No. And then I hate myself for forgiving it. For forgiving him, almost too easily. And not ever being able to forgive myself. Why can I forgive him, but never me? I'm not...I'm not...worth anything anymore, not to anyone, not even me. That's why I have to do this. You see? Because there's nobody else out there that I can trust. I can't even trust myself. Not with this."

She stops and she has no more tears. She stares across the street at the buildings, her gaze distant.

I look down at my hands and think about how helpless I feel right now. There's nothing I can do. I can't fix this. I can't fix any of this. And now I understand why finding Matt Smith is so important to her.

That's something I can do.

"I'll find him," I say. "I'll get you to him in time."

She looks over at me and I wipe the tears from her face.

"I'll find him," I say.

"But Shelly's gone. All our money's gone. Our phones. Everything's gone."

I pull her to my side. "I'll get you to your soul mate. I promise."

I won't let her down again.

21

Nick

WE NEED TO GET TO RACHEL, NEVADA, A TINY SPECK OF A TOWN in the desert about three hours north of Vegas. No one at the furry party is heading that way. I ask everyone in the hotel lobby, all the people coming in and out of the diner next door, and even the hotel workers. No one is heading north. No one.

To get some cash, I pawn my watch for a measly seventy-two dollars. I try to pawn our costumes, but the shop doesn't want them. Chloe and I binge on carrot sticks and hummus at the furry party for a late dinner, then donate our costumes to the cause. Luckily, we were wearing our clothing underneath the fur.

We decide to camp at a gas station near the highway ramp. It has a steady flow of cars fueling up and I approach driver after driver. Most of them flat out tell me no or are suspicious of my motives. But, finally, I find a driver heading north.

His name's Tim. His face is wrinkled and as dry as the Vegas air. He and his wife just had a baby and they and their two pit bulls are headed north to visit the grandparents. Better yet, they have a rusted white pickup truck with an open bed that's just waiting for us to hop into.

"Ain't much," says Tim.

"We can't thank you enough," I say.

He smiles and his face becomes even craggier. "Jus' keep down while I'm driving. I'll try to take 'er easy and not stir up a dust storm in yer faces."

"Thank you so much," says Chloe. She takes Tim's hand and squeezes it. "You have no idea how much this means."

Tim blushes, then looks back at his wife sitting in the truck. She opens the door and shouts, "The baby's fed and changed. All set."

Tim pulls down the tailgate.

I boost Chloe into the truck bed and then hop in after her.

"Y'all ready?" asks Tim.

"Thank you," I say.

He slams the tailgate and climbs into the cab. Chloe and I sit in the truck bed with our backs resting against the window. Tim starts the truck and pulls out of the gas station onto the highway. It's a funny feeling looking over Vegas from the bed of a pickup. The moon is rising to our right, climbing into the arid night. As the sky shifts from blue to black the lights of the hotel casinos wink on. They look like stars, closer to the land, but still wished upon just as much as their counterparts. I know better than most how much.

I don't think the wishes ever come true.

I look over at Chloe. She stares at the city, a deep longing on her face. I wonder if she's making a wish. We're only three hours from the last Matt. If I were a betting man, I'd say she's about to find her soul mate. And I promised I'd get her to him, didn't I?

Suddenly, I hate to leave Vegas. I hate to leave it and I hate to see it fade in the distance. What a turnaround from earlier today. But these next few hours are probably the last Chloe and I will have together. Ever.

Here we are, speeding down a highway in the back of a truck. The wind is so loud that conversation's impossible. But what would I say? What could I say? Choose me?

The dust and the sand in the air stings my eyes and I rub them. Chloe turns to me. I wipe at my eyes and quirk a smile.

Thank you, she mouths.

You're welcome, I say to the wind.

Then I hold out my hand. She looks down then back up and shakes her head no. The wish that I made, to spend the last of our time together holding her hand, vanishes. I let my hand fall. I lean my head against the truck window and stare at the darkening sky. It's that time, when the darkness is here, but there still aren't any stars in sight. The darkest, loneliest time of night. Then I lose a breath as Chloe moves closer, and closer still. Until her thigh presses against my thigh, and her arm presses against my arm, and her shoulder to mine. Everywhere she touches sparks and comes alive. I don't move. I don't even want to breathe. Because I don't want to interrupt the feel of her body on mine. And then, she rests her head against my chest. I draw in a harsh breath. I breathe in the dry sand air that smells like thirst mixed with the perfume of her hair and her skin. My hand shakes as I move my arm and slowly wrap it around her shoulders. Then I pull her in to rest against me. It takes an eternity, but finally, she sinks into me and I hold her.

I hold her like this is both the first time and the last time.

Both heaven and hell.

She watches the city disappear and the stars appear. I watch her. The headlights stroking her skin. The wind brushing through her hair. The expressions drifting across her face as we move farther north.

All this trip, I've been thinking that soul mates aren't real, and that they can't possibly exist. In fact, I set out to prove it. But what if a soul mate is the one person who, when you're with them, there's no place you'd rather be? Because right now, it doesn't matter that I don't have Shelly, or money, or a phone, or that I'm in the back of a truck. None of that matters, because I'm with her. And I can't see that ever changing. Fifty years down the road, there still will be no place I'd rather be.

I pull her closer and lean my head down on top of hers. This is it. The last of it. The end. With every mile we drive, I'm one step closer to losing her.

If there's any wetness in my eyes, no one knows it but me and the wind.

And if there were a thousand miles more to go, not just one hundred, the ending would still be the same. I'd be here, ready to let her go, because I understand now. She needs her soul mate. And like she said...that's not me.

I close my eyes and whisper into her hair, *I love you.*

The wind carries my words away.

22

Chloe

WE TURNED ONTO EXTRATERRESTRIAL HIGHWAY, SPEED LIMIT, warp 7, about forty-five minutes ago. Five minutes ago, we turned onto a wide dirt road. Tim pulls to a stop at the end of a long driveway with a black mailbox. A cloud of dust settles over the truck and then dissipates in the slight breeze. Tim hops out of the truck and comes around to unlatch the tailgate.

Nick and I didn't talk on the ride here, which I'm glad for. I'm confused and starting to question so many things. And here we are, already at our final stop. It's hard to admit, but I was half praying for a flat tire so that we wouldn't make it in time.

Because at the end of this dirt drive is Matt Smith. My soul mate. And then, I'll have to say goodbye to Nick.

The tailgate clatters and Tim breaks into a big smile.

"Y'all do alright?" he asks. "The missus hollered at me the whole darn way. Slow down, she said, watch that bump, she said."

"It was great," I say.

Nick stands and holds out his hand to me. I ignore the little hiccup in my heart. It's just Nick. The bane of my existence. Well, no. That's not right anymore. Too much has changed. But still. It's just Nick. I take his hand and refuse to acknowledge the warmth that curls in my belly at his touch.

"Thank you," I say.

"You're welcome," he says, and his eyes spark. I never noticed this before, but they're not absolute black. There are flecks of gold and hazel and deep brown. His eyes have a thousand dimensions to them. They're an artist's dream.

I shake my head and hop down into the dirt.

Nick jumps down too, then he stretches his arms over his head. I try not to watch, but I can't help but feel more aware of him. Those arms were just around me. I was just laying against his chest. I know how hard and warm it is.

He turns to Tim and holds out his hand for a firm handshake. "Thank you again. I can't express how much I appreciate it."

Tim laughs, "Nothing to it. Good luck to you and yer missus."

I shake my head. "He's not—"

"Thank you," says Nick.

I wave as Tim climbs into his truck and drives off in a cloud of desert dust. "Why'd you let him think we were together?" I ask.

"Does it matter?"

I look down at my shoes. They sink into the coarse sand. Tim's headlights fade and we're left in the dark. "Guess not," I say.

I look around at where we were dropped. This is the location of the last Matt Smith. About a quarter mile down the driveway is a silver trailer. There are maybe two dozen satellite dishes on the roof of and around the trailer. There's one large dish that is bigger than the trailer sitting in the front yard. I didn't realize it before we drove in, but we're just outside Area 51. Aliens are a big deal here. I glance between the trailer and the satellite dishes pointing at the sky. Apparently Matt Smith is a *believer*.

There isn't another house, building, or trailer as far as I can see. There's just dirt, sand, and more sand. It's an ugly place with a strange feeling. It's like all the nuclear testing done around here has stuck in the soil and you can feel it. Like you're squatting underneath a hundred high-voltage electric wires. I shiver and rub my hands up and down my arms.

The stars are out, I can hear the night bugs and the sound of a car, maybe Tim's truck far in the distance. Otherwise, there's only me, Nick, and Matt Smith in his trailer. The lights are on and I can see a TV screen flickering through the window.

I turn to Nick and search his face, but I can't read his expression. I silently urge him to tell me that this is all bull crap, that soul mates aren't real, and that he's taking us back to New York. But, for the first time on this trip, he doesn't.

"Come on, Sparky. Don't lose your spunk now."

I look up at him and see that he's trying his best to help me go forward. Even when it looks like my soul mate is an alien conspiracist.

I let out a long sigh and my shoulders fall. "Why?" I gesture to the thirty gazillion satellites. "Wouldn't this be a good time to remind me that soul mates aren't real and that I should give up? Look at this place. You can tell me you were right."

Honestly, maybe he should.

He shakes his head. "No. I wasn't right. You need this."

We stare at each other. I look into his eyes as they reflect the stars, and he looks into mine. We stand in the sand, not speaking, and not moving, just staring. We're an odd pair. Completely, totally insane. If I were brave, I'd tell him how I feel.

But I'm not brave.

Here's the thing. Everyone thinks that someone is brave if they run into a fire or stop a robbery or save someone. Sure, that's brave. But it doesn't take much thought, it just takes action. There's no time for thinking, you act on instinct—pure emotion. Just like falling in love. The first time, you just do it. You dive in head first and fall. There isn't any thought about a crash or about you being broken.

So, here is what it means to have courage.

After you run into a fire, and it melts your skin and burns your lungs, and someone dies, and you see the horror and feel the pain...after that, you find out that you have to go back in again. But this time, you know the pain and you know the horror...going back in the second time, that's courage.

I understand now what loving someone can do to you. I've been in that fire and I've felt the pain. I'm not brave. I'm not strong enough to go there again unless I know it's safe. Love isn't safe. Do you see? I'm not brave enough to go there without a guarantee.

Apparently, I'm a coward who can only be with a stranger in a trailer in the desert.

Nick reaches out and wipes a tear from my cheek that I didn't realize was falling.

"It'll work out," he says. "Remember? Your aunt hasn't failed anyone yet. Much less her own niece. You'll be alright."

I nod and sniff back more tears. "Yeah. It'll be alright," I say. "Can I hold your hand 'til we get there?"

"Always, Sparky."

He holds his hand out to me and I take it. Then we walk down the dirt driveway. The sand and rocks crunch and give way beneath our feet as the dark swallows us. I wish that I'd never started this trip, and that I never started looking for my soul mate.

Except, that's not quite right. Because then, I wouldn't be here holding Nick's hand. We step up to the door of the silver trailer, an Airstream. I let go of Nick's hand and knock.

23

Nick

MATT SMITH NUMBER SIX...

THIS MATT SMITH IS PROBABLY THE SMARTEST PERSON I'VE EVER met. I mean, this guy is off-the-charts Stephen Hawking smart. He has thick brown hair and a cowlick. *Jeopardy* is muted on the television and he calls out the answer to every question in the middle of our conversation. We're sitting at his tiny dining room table drinking day-old coffee.

He drums his fingers on the table. "Allow me to clarify," he says. "You are searching for Matthew Smith?"

Chloe nods.

"Out of the 9,613 in the United States you narrowed the number down to 364, then 27, then six, of which I am one?"

Chloe nods again.

"Do you realize the probability of you reaching the correct Matthew Smith is point zero, zero, zero, zero, zero—"

"Um," says Chloe.

"Zero, zero one."

"Okay?" says Chloe. It comes out like a long drawn out question. Because, from the second he started talking, neither of us quite followed what he was saying.

Matt answered the door after Chloe's first knock. He looked around, completely paranoid, and yanked us inside. His trailer is piled with newspaper articles, journal articles, and maps. There are six computers running, what looks like a server room, and an air-conditioning unit. There's a small cot with a brown blanket, but I don't think the guy sleeps much, judging by his bloodshot eyes and heavy bags.

"Did you go to summer camp in New York?" asks Chloe.

"Why narrow it to me?" he asks. He taps his fingers on the table, then fidgets with his coffee cup.

"You were the right demographic," I say.

"What is Cleveland?" says Matt.

"What?" I ask. But then I realize he's talking to the TV.

He turns back to me and leans forward. His eyes narrow. "Did *they* send you?"

"Who?" I ask.

"*They.*"

Chloe shifts in her seat. "Um. See, my aunt is psychic."

Matt turns to her and tilts his head. His cowlick bobs. "To clarify, how does the precognition manifest?"

"She can see soul mates," says Chloe.

"What is her success ratio?"

"Um, one hundred percent," says Chloe.

Matt's hand stills on his mug. "What is thirty-six?"

"No. One hundred," says Chloe.

I turn to the TV. The answer is revealed as thirty-six. He's right again.

The show goes to commercial break and Matt turns back to the table. Chloe leans forward, her face earnest.

"Please. You're the last Matt Smith and my aunt promised I'd find my soul mate on this trip. I only have one more day until my time runs out. Please. I need to know."

Matt tilts his head and studies Chloe like she's a complicated puzzle he needs to solve. His fingers twitch on the mug.

"Did you know, the statistics of soul mates make them highly improbable? Your chance of discovering yours are once in every ten thousand lifetimes." It's like he's reciting a universal law that's irrefutable.

Chloe shakes her head, a slow back and forth movement of denial. "I don't agree."

"You don't have to agree with a fact to make it true. That's the beauty of facts. What are the Pentagon Papers?"

I look at the TV, it's the final round.

Chloe puts both her hands on the table and leans toward Matt. "You don't have to agree with the idea of soul mates for it to be true, that's the beauty of fate," she says.

Matt leans back in his chair and finally, really looks at the both of us. "To clarify, your soul mate is named Matt Smith?"

"Yes," says Chloe.

"To clarify, he's from New York, he grew up near Utica, and he went to summer camp with you?"

"And he was my first kiss."

Matt drums his fingers on the table and gives me a speculative look. "I'm from New York," he says. "I grew up near Utica."

There's a sharp pinch in my chest.

"I went to summer camp," he says.

The sharp pinch becomes a knife. This is the moment. I look at Chloe and silently try to get her to look back at me. But she won't. She can't take her eyes off Matt Smith.

"And?" she asks.

"Who is Ernest Hemingway?" asks Matt.

"And?" I growl.

He turns back to Chloe. "I never kissed you," he says.

Thank god.

I turn to see how Chloe is taking the news. She's stunned. I make to reach out to her, but suddenly, a long blaring alarm sounds inside the trailer. I jump at the noise. Then, the trailer plunges into darkness. A second later an eerie red light starts flashing. I grab Chloe and scramble back from the table.

"What is that?" I ask.

"It's *them*," Matt says. "They're here."

That's when I know...Colorado has *nothing* on the outskirts of Area 51.

24

Chloe

MATT RUNS FROM ONE COMPUTER TO THE NEXT AND FRANTICALLY types in commands. It's only been twenty seconds since the alarm started but he's nearly through all six computers. Nick positioned himself so that he's standing between me and Matt, who's clearly gone off the deep end.

"Them who?" I ask.

Nick shakes his head at me with a "don't engage the crazy" look. He motions toward the door and I nod. That's a good idea. We should leave. Even if we have to walk through a desert for a couple miles to get back to that alien gift shop we saw.

Oh. Ohhh. *Them.*

"The aliens are here?" I ask. Because...I have to know. Because...aliens.

Matt frantically rips papers from his walls and throws them into a metal bin. While he shoves reams of paper into the container, he looks at me like I've lost my mind. "Are you insane? Haven't you read the Fermi Paradox? Aliens aren't real."

Oookay. Then, who's *them*? Matt pulls out some sort of metal ball. Nick swears and shoves me into the wall. There's a loud bang, like an explosion.

Panic fills me and I scream.

Nick covers my entire body. I scream again. He shakes me and I turn around. There's ringing in my ears and an acrid smoke smell in the room.

Matt stands over a smoking metal bin, the papers are now burnt black char.

"We're going," says Nick.

He grabs me and starts for the door.

"Don't," says Matt, "don't go out that door."

"Try and stop us," says Nick. But then I pull at his hand because that's...yeah, that's an automatic gun I hear.

Nick hears it too, because he stops and turns to Matt.

"What is this?" he asks.

Matt grabs a backpack from under a computer. Then he charges toward the cot. He puts his fingerprint on a scanner on the wall and the cot flips up to reveal a trap door in the floor. He yanks it open and jumps down.

"Come on," Matt says.

The sound of gunfire decides it for me. I jump into the scary hole in the ground and land on a compact dirt floor. I step forward and Nick jumps down after me. Matt uses another fingerprint scanner on the wall and the trapdoor closes. We're in a short concrete tunnel that's lit by dim red lights on the walls. It stretches forward. Matt starts to run. I look at Nick.

"Let's go," he says.

We both take off after Matt. He sprints like his life depends on it, so I decide to do the same. Nick has to hunch over. The tunnel is barely tall enough for me to stand in. I run over the hardpacked dirt and hit my hands against the tight concrete walls. My heart pounds and I suck in the musty uncirculated air. The tunnel stays straight, and doesn't slant up or down. After about half a mile we stop at a dead end. I bend over and drag in a lungful of air.

"What is this?" asks Nick.

There's a metal ladder bolted in the wall that leads up to another door in the ceiling. Matt scans his fingerprint again and the hatch opens. He climbs the ladder and peeks out. At that moment, a loud explosion rips through the air.

Matt loses his hand hold and falls to the hard dirt floor. "They destroyed my Airstream," he says.

Nick pulls Matt to his feet. "Explosives?"

Matt nods. "Kablooey. They'll find this tunnel. We need to evacuate."

"Who is they?" I ask. Clearly, *they* are not aliens.

Matt looks at me like I'm dense. "The Mafia. We're in Nevada. Who did you think?"

He climbs up the ladder and slowly pokes his head out. "We're clear," he whispers.

"I'll go first," says Nick, "Don't come up until I say it's okay."

I nod and watch as his legs disappear. Almost right away he reappears and motions me up. I climb the ladder and come out into the night. The trailer is a huge ball of fire. I can see three cars parked near the blaze, and I can make out three, no four figures walking around the perimeter.

Matt pulls up a tarp. "Give me a hand," he says.

Nick grabs one of the edges and they pull the tarp away to reveal a twenty foot by ten foot dugout. Parked inside is a monster truck. Matt Smith has a monster truck in a hole in the desert.

"Get in," he says. He's already jumped down.

"They're coming," says Nick. He points to the Town Cars.

They've seen us and are speeding this way. I don't know what they'll do if they catch us. But I don't want to wait around to find out. I've never heard a story where the Mafia guys let the witnesses go.

I jump down into the dugout and Nick follows. We hop into the monster truck. Matt roars the truck to life and revs out of the dugout. It jumps into the air and lands in the sand. Matt punches the gas. I look behind us.

"They're gaining on us," I say.

I look over at Nick. His jaw is hard and he looks pissed. "I just *had* to get you to him, didn't I?"

I roll my eyes. "Didn't you know…I've always wanted to ride in a monster truck."

We hit a small hill and the monster truck goes airborne. My stomach goes up and then slams down as we hit the ground. The three black cars are close. Their headlights shine in the back window.

"Please don't die, please don't die," I whisper.

Ahead of us is a ravine. It's big, and there's a drop, I don't know how deep. We're headed straight for it.

"Turn," I say. "Ditch. Big ditch."

Matt guns the engine. We're only a hundred feet from the ravine. "Turn. Please turn."

We're going to plunge to our deaths with a lunatic.

"Turn."

"Trust science," says Matt.

He hits a button on the dash and a metal ramp lifts from the sand. The headlights glint off it. Oh no. Oh no. I changed my mind. I never, ever want to ride in a monster truck again.

Matt guns it.

Nick grabs my hand. I brace myself as we hit the ramp. We fly into the air. We hang above the ravine. It feels like an eternity even though we're still moving. Then, just as suddenly as we went up, we crash to the other side of the chasm. We land.

I whoop. I scream and holler and hug Nick. I climb onto him and hug him and laugh.

"We made it. We made it." I hang onto him like a maniac that'll never let go.

Matt pushes the button on the dash. I look back. The three cars are stopped at the edge of the ravine. They aren't going to catch us. I hug Nick harder.

"We made it," I say again.

Nick scowls down at me, a glint in his eyes. "It'll be fun, she said. They'll all be perfectly normal rich lumberjacks, she said."

I laugh and nuzzle into him. Finally, my heart stops racing enough for me to climb off Nick's lap.

"Where are we going?" I ask Matt.

"To my safe house in Death Valley. You can stay the night."

"Thank you," I say. I turn to Nick and give him a wide-eyed *Noooooo* stare.

"Maybe you could drop us at an inexpensive motel instead?" Nick asks.

So, once we're back on a road and to a small crossroads sort of town, Matt leaves us at a roadside motel. I thank him for saving our lives and for the ride. Then, Nick and I go get a room to share.

25

Nick

One Day Left...

I PAY FIFTY-NINE DOLLARS AND SEVENTY CENTS FOR A ROOM AT the Death Valley Motor Inn and Motel. The billboard on the roadside advertised cable tv, air conditioning and running water. Death Valley receives less rainfall than any other place in the U.S., and from what I can see, it looks like another planet. Mars, maybe. There are strangely sloping hills that look like piles of tan pulled taffy and miles of dry, cracked nothingness.

We have twelve dollars and thirty cents left, no car, no phones, and we're in a place that looks like the aftermath of the apocalypse.

The motel was most likely built in the fifties, it's single story, was probably once brown, but is now sun faded to tannish gray. There are twelve rooms. We're in number eight. I unlock the door with an old metal key on a key chain that says, *Death Valley, You Made It.*

The hinges squeak as I swing the door open. I step inside and flip on the lights. Chloe comes in after me and I shut and lock the door behind her. The room is a lot nicer than I anticipated. It smells like Dove soap and lemon polish. There's a double bed with white linens tuckpointed into the corners. A cushy brown recliner is angled near the window.

"I'll take the recliner," I say.

She turns to me. "Don't be ridiculous."

I take a moment to study her. I've been avoiding it. It's two a.m. on day seven and we've gone through all the Matt Smith candidates. It's over. We failed. Chloe didn't find her soul mate. Back in Vegas, I promised her that we'd get to him and we didn't. I failed.

The part I don't want to admit, though, is that I'm glad. There's a bright hope growing inside of me. If she doesn't find him, then maybe she'll find that I can be who she needs. I'm not perfect, I may not be her soul mate, but I love her, and I could spend the rest of my life showing her how much.

She settles down on the bed, props up the pillows and leans back against the headboard.

"Can I join you?" I ask.

She pats the space next to her. I sink onto the bed, it's old and soft and dips toward the middle. I lean back and relax into the softness. It feels like a miracle sitting here next to her, when hours ago, I thought she'd be gone for good. We're cocooned in the quiet of the room and the only sound is the soft hum of the air conditioning.

Chloe's eyes focus on someplace distant, either in the past or her imagined future. But, wherever she's at, it's not here with me.

"Penny for your thoughts?" I ask. "But only a penny, because we're broke."

She gives a short laugh and turns to me. When she shakes her head I have the sudden urge to reach out and stroke the curls falling over her shoulders.

"I was just thinking that maybe we missed one. Maybe there's another Matt," she says.

All that glowing hope inside me gutters out. I look away for a moment and pull myself back into reality. The reality where Chloe desperately wants to find and marry a man she hasn't seen in twenty years.

"Yeah," I say. My voice cracks. I try again. "Yeah. Let me call Reed. Maybe he's found something since we left Romeo." He may have discovered a lead or found a Matt that we missed in our initial search.

Chloe's eyes light with hope. Why wouldn't they? We still have twenty odd hours to find her soul mate. I turn my back and close my eyes. Then I pick up the beige receiver of the hotel phone and make a collect call. It's five in the morning in New York and I'm sure Reed's already up. I don't know whether to laugh or cry when Reed picks up and then confirms that there are no more Matt Smiths on the radar. I thank him and hang up.

When I look over at Chloe, I can tell that she got the gist of the conversation.

"So, it's over," she says. Her shoulders slump and her chin falls to her chest. "I thought..." She stops and turns to me. "My aunt said I had to find him before the week was up. She said I would. I thought..."

"We tried," I say. But it sounds lame in the light of the sadness in her eyes. I think about what she shared in Vegas. I know from experience, it sucks to love someone and have them hurt you so much.

"Do you remember the first time we made love?" I ask.

Chloe's head jerks up and her cheeks turn red. "Aunt Erma said first kiss, not first sex."

I keep going even though a heavy weight presses on my chest. This is important. I scoot closer to her until we're touching. "I let a misunderstanding keep me away from you for ten years. Maybe I needed to grow up until I could be the man you'd need."

"Nick..." she says. She starts to move away.

"Listen, this is important."

She closes her eyes and her lower lip trembles. "Okay."

Hesitantly I take her hand and start to stroke the back of it. "I've been thinking."

"Yeah?" A small smile lights on her lips.

"Yeah, Sparky. About us."

She licks her lips and looks at me with trepidation. "We're not..."

"Hang on. This is important." I take both her hands in mine. "You always believed that soul mates are decided by fate, right?"

She nods.

"And I thought soul mates didn't exist."

"Yeah, you win. I didn't find mine. I didn't prove you wrong."

"No. That's just it. You did."

She shakes her head. "How?"

"Because I realize I always believed in soul mates. Just not the kind you do. What if two people can become soul mates?"

"What?"

I lean forward and squeeze her hands. I've been mulling this over and I think I'm right. "What if two people become soul mates by growing and fitting together? What if fate doesn't decide soul mates, what if we create our own?"

I silently beg her to give this idea a chance. It takes what feels like a thousand years for her to respond. I've just jumped off the edge of a high cliff and she can either catch me or let me fall. She looks down at our joined hands. They fit perfectly together.

Then, "Like you and me?" she asks.

Thank the lord.

"Like you and me," I say.

"I'm scared," she whispers.

Me too.

If we'd really talked all those years ago, then she never would've dated Ron, and she never would've been hurt. I would already be her husband and we might already have children. I loved her all those years ago and if I'd stayed with her, I would've married her. No doubt about it. There wouldn't be any question of soul mates. She'd be mine and I'd be hers. Now, I see a future where *we* might never be, and that terrifies me.

"Me too," I say.

She looks up sharply and takes in my expression. "You are?"

I nod. "Remember how you said it takes bravery to fall in love after you realize there's a bottom?"

"Yes?"

"We could fall together, and if we crash, I'll let you land on top of my body."

She laughs and wipes at her eyes. "That's not how it's supposed to be. Soul mates are in unison, in perfect sync. They have lots in common and they get each other. It's like two souls that were torn apart and when they find each other again they're whole."

"But what if we go through life and become whole together? You don't start out like that, you become that. I could become yours. You could be mine."

This is it, my impassioned plea. That maybe, at the eleventh hour, Chloe will find her soul mate—in me.

"And the first kiss?" she asks. Earlier, she looked scared, now there's something else there. An echoing of hope, maybe?

I nod. "Yes."

"Yes?"

"Yes." I lean forward and press my lips to hers. Her mouth is like a fresh spring in the desert, sweet, cool and enough to bring a man back to life.

"That's not—" she says against my mouth.

I press my lips to hers and silence her protest.

"Watch," I say.

I lean down and gently move her sleeves down her shoulders. I press my lips to her collarbone. I trace them over her warmth and linger over her scent. "This," I say, "is the first kiss to your collarbone." I pull her top lower and press my mouth over her shoulder. "This is the first kiss to your shoulder." She gasps at the feel of my mouth. I take her dress and push it down. I send my mouth over her skin. "The first kiss to your ribs. The first kiss to the underside of your breast."

I look up at her when I reach her bra. Her eyes have gone heavy and have taken on her horny "thinking of my soul mate" look, but this time, I know it's for me.

"Yes?" I ask.

"Yes," she says.

I unstrap her bra and my fingers linger on the curve of her spine. I suck on her nipple and run my tongue over it. Then, I move to the other and suckle it as her fingers run through my hair and urge me on. I splay my hands across her stomach and trail my mouth over her skin.

"First kiss," I say.

I watch her face as I slowly push down her skirt. Her eyes are on the space where my fingers meet her hip bones.

"Yes?" I ask.

"Yes," she says.

I pull her dress off and let the smooth fabric trace over her. She reclines back on the bed, her hair spread around her, only in her panties. I suck on the skin above her hipbone. "First kiss." Her face is flushed and her skin is glowing. When I look up at her I see that her eyes are full of heat. Like a man possessed, I bend back to her and kiss my way over her skin. I recite each place on her body from the tip of her pinky to the dip where her neck meets the curve of her jaw.

"Your eyebrows," I say as I place a kiss. "Your eyelashes. These fairy kisses on your inner thigh that look like a constellation. First kiss." I pull her thighs apart and knead them. I trail my lips up and make sure to cover every inch of skin. "First kiss."

"These aren't all first kisses," she says. Her voice is teasing and full of the devil, and that's when I know, she's saying...yes.

I take her panties and we both watch as I pull the rough lace over her thighs and down her calves and then drop them to the bed. I lower myself back to her and she runs her fingers through my hair.

"But this is?" I ask.

"This is," she says.

I smile and press my mouth over her clit. I take it in my mouth and run my tongue over her, savoring her taste and her cries. I move over her and explore her, inside and out. When I move back up to her clit, she lifts her hips and cries out. I suck on her and pull harder, until she's bucking under me and crying out. When she falls back to the bed I look up. "First kiss."

When she looks at me, her eyes are hungry and no longer sad. Just happy. From my kiss.

"Definitely," she says. "That was definitely, absolutely my first kiss."

My heart thunders in my chest. She reads the look on my face and holds her arms open to me.

"Can I have another?" she asks.

"Yeah?" I ask. Suddenly, stunned at the turn events. Does she mean it?

"What are you waiting for?" she asks.

I growl and tear off my clothes. In seconds, we're both naked. I climb on top of her and use my knees to part her thighs. I brace myself above her and rub my length along her. The feel of her warmth is heaven and I want nothing more than to plunge inside her. Make her mine. I bring my mouth to hers and taste her sweetness. I run along her entrance while she teases me with her hips, arching and inviting me in then pulling away. I run my tongue into her mouth and she sucks on my lips. I would kiss her forever. I never want this to stop. She arches up again and the tip of me barely enters her tight warmth. My body ignites with feeling, and I want so bad to push in all the way. I grit my teeth and she cries out into my mouth. With all of my willpower I pull back and instead run along her wet entrance.

"This is okay?" I ask. "You want this?"

I look down at her and I swear to God, I've never seen anything so beautiful in my whole life.

"Yes," she says. "Yes."

We stare into each other's eyes. I fall into her gaze and what I see there makes me feel whole. The whole world disappears. It's only us. Slowly, I move over her entrance and push into her. Inch by excruciating inch, I'm buried inside her. Her heat wraps around me and holds me tight. A drop of sweat drips down my brow. I'm drowning in her. I keep pushing in, as deep

166

and as far as I can go, until I'm so deep inside her I've lost track of where I end and she begins.

She gasps and pulls me closer. Her arms wrap over my shoulders and her legs around my thighs. I pull in a sharp breath and give in to the overwhelming urge to move. I pull back, and feel like I've lost the universe, so I plunge back in her and feel like I've come home. As I pull out, I feel lost. So, again and again, I pull out and push in. I lose the universe only to find it again.

Her eyes are changing color, becoming a darker shade. Her pupils have almost swallowed the color entirely. I press my forehead to hers and plunge in again.

"Nick," she says, and I catch her cry with my kiss.

"Cum," I say.

I want to feel her.

"Cum."

"You," she says.

I smile. Even in this, she has to fight me. I reach down and run my fingers over her clit as I move inside her. I stroke her and pet her.

"Come for me," I say. "Let me feel you."

When she looks up at me, I try to convey that she can trust me. That I won't hurt her. That I'll always do what's best and what's right.

"Yes," she cries.

Then, I feel her clench around me. She clasps my length inside her and the strength of her orgasm pulls me deeper in. My whole being fills with her, and I have to move. I have to, I have to fill her too. I thrust into her as she convulses around me. White sparks light in my eyes as pressure fills the base of my length. It grows and grows until I can't feel anything but her and the need to be inside her. Always.

She convulses around me and her grip is so tight and

demanding that I can't do anything but obey. I shout out and push in harder and deeper. I try with all my soul and all my might to bring us both to heaven. To bring our two souls together. I cum in her, long and hard, and when I do, I know, I know with absolute certainty that she is mine.

When the last of her orgasm fades, I roll to my back and pull her onto me. Then, I kiss her forehead, her cheeks, her eyelashes and the tip of her nose. She snuggles into me and buries her face into my shoulder. This, unequivocally, is the best day of my life. Nothing can ruin it.

"Thank you," I say.

"For what?" she says sleepily.

I squeeze her to me, wondering if it's too soon to do it again. Or if it's too soon to tell her I love her?

Chloe dozes off and I stare at the ceiling, lost in thought. In less than twenty hours the week is over. We'll go home. I failed Erma's job, so I won't get my payment—the land and the cabin. But it doesn't matter anymore. I've gotten something infinitely better.

I fall asleep to the sound of Chloe's breathing.

It's only five hours later that I'm pulled from sleep. Chloe's answered the phone.

"Hello?"

I hear a man's voice on the other end. "Chloe? It's Matthew, from last night. To clarify, I'm the Matthew—"

"Right, I know who you are," she says sleepily.

"Chloe, I found him. I found your Matt Smith. Can you believe it? He's in L.A. His name is Matthias—"

He's still talking, but I can't hear him anymore. I'm watching Chloe's face. There's a thousand emotions there. I catalog them all. Disbelief, shock, confusion, dismay, hope, then, the worst emotion of all, the nail in the coffin—joy. Her face fills with joy.

26

Chloe

TIME'S UP...

NICK AND I STAND IN FRONT OF THE MOST BEAUTIFUL HOUSE I'VE ever seen. I'm pretty sure it was on the cover of *Architectural Digest* a few issues back. I stare at the three-story home built mostly of windows and wood beams. It's perched on a cliff with an expansive view of the Pacific Ocean. I can smell the salty water and hear the gulls and the waves. I've never seen so much perfection in one setting.

This is Matthias Smith's house. My Matt Smith.

The sun reflects off the windows and I squint into the glare. We're in a suburb of Los Angeles known for its expensive homes, open space, beachfront and stunning views of the ocean.

Number Six, as Nick calls him, drove us here. He has

access to some serious databases, and after heading to his safe house last night, he decided to do some research on my soul mate story. He found the real Matt Smith, and since he felt bad about endangering our lives, he offered to drive us to LA.

"Are you sure about this?" I ask Nick.

He runs his hand down the back of his neck. When he turns to me he has a rueful smile on his face. "Promised I'd get you here, didn't I?"

I look into his eyes and see all the colors I've come to love. Gold, hazel, deep brown, black. Last night, I felt like I could feel his soul, but now, I can't read him.

"You did," I say, "But..."

He shakes his head. "But what?"

"What if we just go home?" I ask.

Number Six left right after dropping us off. We don't have any money left. We don't have any time. It's the late afternoon of the last day to find my soul mate. I thought that maybe Nick was right and we create our own soul mates. Except, here we are. Fate pulled through and we found the man that I really first kissed. He's inside the beautiful mansion only fifty feet away. My Aunt Erma predicted it and it's come to pass. She's never wrong.

My heart squeezes. She isn't.

Nick reaches over and wipes my cheek.

"Don't cry, Sparky."

I choke out a laugh. "I never asked, why do you call me that?"

He shakes his head and looks away, out over the ocean.

"No you don't, Nick O'Shea. After all we've been through, you'll tell me why you gave me that stupid nickname."

He turns back and I catch my breath at the look on his face.

"Because," he says, "when I first realized I wanted you, it

was like getting hit by an electric shock. Hurt like hell, but it was necessary to restart my heart."

I step back, completely and utterly confused. "But you've called me that for almost twenty years. You—" I finally connect the dots. He's loved me...for years.

I look at the house again. "Let's go back to New York," I say.

I ignore the fear and the complete and utter terror of trusting my future to an unknown and going against my aunt's prediction. Matt Smith is guaranteed as my soul mate to never hurt me. Can the same be said of Nick?

My heart cries out, yes. Can it?

He's watching me carefully. Then his jaw tightens and his eyes darken.

"I promised your aunt I'd get you to your soul mate. I promised you too."

Why does this hurt so much? I step toward Nick and close the distance between us. "Okay. Fine. We're here. Promise complete."

He shakes his head and nods toward the mansion. "Let's go meet the guy you were born for. Lucky Number Seven."

I look down at my feet and then at the wrinkled dirty dress I'm wearing. I'm a complete mess. Post furry, post car chase, post best sex of my life.

"I'm sorry," I whisper, my heart breaking. Because we both know that I'm going to do it. Even after last night, after everything we've been through, I'm still going to walk ahead and knock on Matt Smith's door.

Because that's what a believer of soul mates, fate and true love does. I dig my nails into my palms.

"Nothing to be sorry for," Nick says, "I shouldn't have done what I did."

"Don't say that."

"It's true. That's the thing about facts. They're true even if you don't believe them," he says, quoting Matt Smith Number Six.

I'm surprised he can joke about this.

"We're not meant to be," I say. It's a question, but it comes out as a statement.

Nick rubs the center of his chest and silence hangs between us. I wait for his response although I'm not sure what I expect him to say.

"Do you hate me?" I ask. Because right now I hate me. I'm scared of Nick. Terrified of him. Because what if I do love him back and what if...a thousand what ifs. Last night I felt closer to him than I've ever felt to anyone in my life. And being that vulnerable without certainty...

Finally, he nods toward the front door of Matt's house. "Come on. Fifty bucks says he's shagging a goat in the living room."

"Weirdo," I say. A warmth grows in my belly. I love him.

He raises an eyebrow. "Wouldn't be the freakiest thing I've seen this week."

I smile at him and he grins down at me. But behind his smile I see something else, the knowledge that it's all over. We're over.

So what do we do?

I take his hand and we walk up to the front door to meet Matt Smith.

For the very last time.

27

Nick

MATT SMITH NUMBER SEVEN, AKA THE REAL DEAL

MATT SMITH IS SIX FOOT TALL. HE HAS BLUE EYES, SHOULDER-length blonde hair and a tan. He opens the door on the first knock. When he sees Chloe he breaks into a huge smile. He has the whitest teeth I've ever seen.

"I know you," he says. He points at Chloe and slowly shakes his head. "We've met before, haven't we?"

I watch Chloe soak up the splendor of Matt Smith Number Seven, aka the Real Deal. She melts as she takes in his charm, his good looks, and his smile. I swear there are hearts floating above her head and she's about to break into song.

"We went to summer camp together," she says.

"Pine Hill," says Matt. He looks Chloe up and down, from

her softly curling hair to her generous mouth. He's making the connection. I see it when he stops on her lips.

"Chloe Daniels," he breathes.

"You remember me?"

"Of course," Matt says. "Come in. Come in." He holds open the brass door to his entryway. We step onto white marble floors. Low leather couches and modern chrome side tables decorate the living room. The furnishings are minimal so as not to detract from the floor-to-ceiling windows looking over the ocean.

Matt leads us to the couches and offers us a seat.

"I can't believe after all these years. Here you are...Chloe Daniels."

I don't like how he says her name. It's as if he's rediscovered his favorite candy from childhood and he's about to settle in for a good long snack.

"And you are, I'm sorry, I don't remember you," Matt says to me. He's sizing me up and wondering if I'm competition.

"He's my b—"

"Friend," I say, not letting her finish. "Nick O'Shea." I hold out my hand and lean across the glass coffee table. Matt shakes. He has a firm, respectable grip.

"So, Chloe Daniels," Matt says, "what are you doing in LA? The last time I saw you was behind the art shed at camp."

She blushes.

If Chloe were to take out her sketch pad and draw this scene, she and Matt would be in a ray of sunshine and I'd be under that lone gray rain cloud. Hell.

I stare out the window at the gray and navy water. The waves are a lot bigger than any I've seen on the east coast. Chloe and Matt keep talking. Minutes pass. She scoots closer to him. He's enthralled with her and hangs on her every word.

Out of the corner of my eye I see him reach out and carefully touch the corner of her hand.

Pull away, I think. Pull away.

She doesn't.

They keep talking. She leans toward him and gives him the smile that I'd started to think of as my own. The one she reserved just for me. They move closer so that their knees touch. He starts to laugh and she brushes the hair from her face. I turn back to the waves. They have so much turmoil, the crest, the froth, the angry dip.

I turn back to Matt and Chloe. They are smiling at each other and completely at ease. I tune into their conversation.

"I love illustrating. I get lost in my drawings for hours," Chloe says.

Matt nods and pats her hand. "I understand. I'll paint from morning until night and forget to eat."

"Exactly," says Chloe. "Me too."

Matt watches her mouth, then says, "it's like I've known you forever. We click."

I stand up so quickly that they both stop talking and look over at me. By their expressions I think they'd forgotten I was in the room.

"Sorry, leg cramp." I rub at my thigh.

"No worries. We were probably boring you. Unless, are you an artist too?" Matt asks.

"I'm a P.I." I say.

"Nick was in the military," Chloe says.

I look at her, but she's not looking at me.

"Nice, man. Thanks for your service."

"You're welcome," I say. It comes out stiffer than I intended.

Matt looks between Chloe and me, then comes to a decision. "I know this may be forward, but I feel like we connect," he says.

Chloe nods. I look away.

Matt continues. "I'm throwing a party here for some friends the next few days. Would you be able to come? It's casual. Grilling out, swimming in the pool, that kind of thing. I'd love to see more of you."

No.

"We'd love to," says Chloe.

No.

"Nick?" asks Matt.

"Sounds good."

Thirty minutes later we know all about Matt. He started an app when he was in college where artists can sell their work. He made millions. Now he runs an artist in residence fellowship where struggling painters, sculptors, textile artists, et cetera can come and work on their art while he provides the housing, the food, and the supplies. He loves his family. He has two rescue dogs. He spends a month every summer helping build schools in third world countries. He's also single and looking for the right person to come along. More than that, he's a nice guy. As much as I want him not to be, so that Chloe and I could bust out of here, I can't deny that Matt Smith is a genuinely good person.

This is the guy that fate chose for Chloe. If I'd been fate I would've chosen him too. He's not cynical, he's not scarred by life, he's one of those rare people that makes everyone happy just by being in the same room. It's time to get my head out of my butt and stop feeling sorry for myself.

After hearing about Vegas, Matt lets me use his phone. I call Reed and explain the situation. As my best friend, he agrees to spot me some cash until I can get back home. Matt drives us to Western Union where Reed wired enough money for Chloe and me to get back to New York. Then, Matt drops us at a nearby hotel. He makes Chloe promise that she'll be there.

The silence of the hotel room is especially loud after Chloe and Matt's talking and laughing of the last few hours. We both look at the king bed covered in pristine white sheets. I think of how far away last night seems now that we've met the real Matt Smith.

I cut into the silence. "He's a good guy."

"He is."

"I guess your Aunt Erma was right." The words taste like ashes.

"She's always right."

There's a lump in my throat and I don't think I can speak past it. Instead, I reach out and touch her hand. A pulse inside me tries to grow, it wants to rage, but I push it back.

"What if Erma's not right? What if he's not—"

"Don't." She pulls her hand away.

But that roaring rage that I pushed back comes to the surface and I can't not. "What if he's not the one?"

"Weren't you there? He's perfect," she says. There's a bitter ache in her voice.

"And I'm not," I say.

She wraps her arms around herself. "I don't know what to do."

All I want to do is hold her.

I pull her down to the bed and fold her in my arms. I rub her back and hold her close. "It's not hard," I say. "On the one hand, you have the perfect man. He's rich, he's an artist, he's good looking and according to your aunt, he's the other half of your soul."

She sniffs and shifts closer.

"On the other hand, you've got a guy who's not rich, who can't draw to save his life, is only passable looking, and isn't your fated destiny." I hold her in my arms and breathe in the scent of her. "There's nothing hard about it at all. See?"

She wraps her arms around my chest. "You're right," she says.

"I always am."

She rests in the cradle of my arms.

"Thank you," she whispers, "I'm not scared anymore."

It hits me then. She's free. She's completely free of the fear of the past and of the future. She doesn't need me anymore. This is goodbye.

I kiss the top of her head and let my lips linger. She sighs and sinks further into my side. As she falls asleep, she sighs, "I choose you."

At first, it feels like the best thing I've ever heard. I want to wake her up and worship her and make love to her. Then, I'd take her to the courthouse and marry her, and tie her to me so she could never leave. That's when my elation crashes to the ground. I want to tie her to me because I'm the one who's scared. Because I realize the truth.

Erma is *never* wrong.

Matt Smith is Chloe's perfect match. I saw the guy, there was no denying it. Matt Smith can make her happy. Wondrously, ecstatically, contentedly happy.

She'll never forgive me if I marry her and don't give her the chance to be with him. She'll say the opposite. She'll claim she wants me, but there will always be a niggle. Like a pebble in her shoe that she can never remove.

I don't want to be that pebble. Even more, I don't want her to settle.

I realize I've been a cynic and I've been selfish. But right now, those are two qualities that are going to serve me well. I'm cynical enough to realize we aren't meant to be. I'm selfish enough to make this choice on my own. I'm leaving so that she can have the life she deserves. I've crossed this invisible threshold where I love her so much that I can't do what I want and what feels good, I have to do what's right.

Leaving and letting her live the life she was destined for is what's right. I guess I'm as deluded as the rest of the folks back home. I get it now.

I'll do whatever it takes, even if it means Chloe might end up hating me in the end. I can't let her lose her chance at happiness. I can be the cynical jerk again to make that happen.

I wait until she falls into a deep sleep then I climb out of the bed. I lay out on the nightstand enough money for the hotel, a car, a plane ticket, clothing, anything she might need. Then I write her a note.

SPARKY, YOU WERE RIGHT. I'M NOT THE ONE AND I NEVER HAVE BEEN. Go to the party and fall in love with your soul mate. You don't need me anymore. I did my part. Nick.

THEN, I LEAVE.

28

Chloe

I WAKE UP WHEN I HEAR THE DOOR CLICK SHUT. I SIT UP IN BED and look around. Something feels wrong.

"Nick?"

No answer.

Then I see a pile of money and a note on the night stand. What it says makes my stomach drop.

I jump up from the bed, shove on my heels, grab the room key and rush out the door. I run down the long corridor until I get to the exit. It's dusk. The night is gray and the streetlights click on as I run into the parking lot. I stand on my tiptoes and see if I can spot Nick. He can't be far. I choose a direction and run past cars and SUVs. Nothing. I turn and run the other way. I have to find him.

A man smokes in front of the hotel entrance, and a couple walks down the sidewalk. An old man lugs a suitcase out of his trunk. A family walks toward the lobby door with their bags. But I don't see Nick anywhere.

I run around to the other side of the hotel parking lot, but it's deserted. Maybe I should run down the sidewalk? I stop and put my hands on my thighs and pull in long breaths. I'm not used to so much running. My heartbeat slows and I straighten up. How could he have left? How he could he?

I doesn't matter. I'll go after him. He left enough money. I'll buy a plane ticket and beat him to New York, since the idiot refuses to fly.

Now that I have a course of action I head back toward the hotel lobby. I need to pack and book a flight. But the door opens before I reach it.

Nick walks out and I stop. He doesn't see me at first. He's looking at the ground. His shoulders are slumped, his head bowed and his hands are in his pockets. If I were designing a card, the caption would say, *I miss you, I need you, I love you.*

I watch him for a moment longer. The idiot. He looks miserable. Then something must alert him to my presence because his head jerks up. When he sees me his eyes go wide and fill with happiness. Pure and undiluted. But just as quickly he slams the emotion down and scowls at me. I'm on to him though, the scowl doesn't fool me at all.

"What are you doing?" he asks.

"Chasing you," I say.

The side of his mouth lifts up, but then he pulls it flat again. "Why?" he asks.

"Because you and I are meant to be. You're right. Soul mates can be created." I watch his reaction. I love his profile. You think, when you first look at him, that he's all hard lines and cynicism, then when you see him from another angle you realize he's really kind, funny, patient, caring, all that and more.

I could draw him for the rest of my life and never capture all the facets that make him unique.

He runs his hand down the back of his neck. "Chloe...I'm going back to New York."

"Then I'll come with you."

He closes his eyes and lets out a long sigh. When he opens his eyes they're hard and dark, with no shining colors inside.

I swallow.

Nick looks around the parking lot. A family comes out the lobby doors.

"Come on," he says.

We walk back to the hotel room. When we get inside he turns to me.

"I'm leaving. I don't want you to come with me."

I shake my head. He has a stubborn look on his face. There's a fear growing inside me, it's rising up in my throat and trying to take over. The more I try to swallow it down, the bigger it gets. Is this the moment? I let him in and now he's going to break my heart?

"Please," I say. "Please stay."

"An hour ago you told me that Matt's perfect. Last night you said that when you meet your soul mate, you feel like you've known them forever and you just click. What did Matt say to you? He said that he felt like he'd known you forever and that the two of you clicked."

"What I said was stupid. It doesn't matter."

"The hell it doesn't."

"It doesn't. I want you."

He takes a step back, like I've struck him. I step toward him. He takes another step back and I take another step forward. His legs hit the bed. He narrows his eyes on me and I push him down. He drops to the edge of the bed.

"Chloe..." he says in a low voice.

I yank the hair tie from my ponytail. Nick watches as my curls fall around my shoulders. He doesn't move away.

"Give me your hands," I say.

He doesn't. So, I take them and he lets me pull them together. Then, I wrap my hair tie around his wrists.

"You're a better sport when you're tied up," I say.

His pupils dilate and the black nearly swallows the brown.

I lean forward and I put my hands on his shoulders. Then I brush my mouth over his lips. He lets out a low sound and I push in harder, crushing my lips against his.

"Admit it," I say, "I'm coming with you."

He shakes his head. "No."

I slant my mouth over his again and run my hands through his hair. When I pull away he has a fierce look in his eyes, one I recognize from the night we made love.

"I'm coming with you," I say.

"Why?"

I pull all my courage around me and remember that I'm not afraid anymore. "Because, I'm...I..."

"Stop," he says.

He looks like he's in pain. I never thought that telling someone I love them would make them look like they've been sucker punched. But I have to try. I *am* brave after all. I'm going to run back into that house, even though it's still on fire and I've been burned before, because I've found my courage. I was brave all along.

I brush his hair away from his forehead and look into his eyes.

"I love you," I say. "I love you so much."

He closes his eyes and his shoulders slump. I wait, and wait, and the longer I wait, the more it hurts. When he opens his eyes, they're not blazing with fire, they're cold. He slowly pulls his hands out of my hair tie and tosses it aside. He stands and moves away.

"A week ago, no, two days ago," he says, "you were ready to marry a stranger you've not seen in decades. You *loved* him. Now you love me? Sorry, Sparky. You don't know what love is." His face is hard and his voice is cold.

"Please, don't do this," I say. "You don't mean it." He can't mean it. Not after last night, or the last week. *He can't.*

He turns away. "What you're feeling are endorphins. From sex. You're confusing lust with love."

I step back, shocked at the bitterness in his voice.

"What's wrong with you?"

"Wrong? I'm the same person I've always been. Remember? *'Love's just a chemical cocktail prepping you for the inevitable hangover.'*" He turns and gives a sardonic smile. "Welcome to the morning after."

Pain bursts in my chest. My hand flies to my heart and I press against the ache there. But I still fight him. "You don't believe that anymore," I say.

"Of course I do. People don't change."

The expression on his face scares me. Is this it? Is this another moment where I give my heart to someone just for them to break it?

"People don't change," I repeat.

"No. They don't."

I remember how he left Romeo all those years ago. He left and he never looked back. "You're always running away," I say, suddenly angry. "You're scared. It's not me who's afraid, it's you. You're leaving again. Don't do this."

He steps closer and looks down into my eyes. At first I think he's going to kiss me, his mouth softens and he leans forward. I think he's going to forget the stupidity of leaving and kiss me.

Instead, he slowly and deliberately says, "I don't want you. It was just sex."

"Liar," I say.

"No. I'm just proving you right. The only person who won't let you down is your soul mate. And that's not me."

"You love me," I say.

He looks down at the floor. "I don't," he says.

"You can't look at me and say that."

I see it in his eyes before he says it and I know that I was wrong. About everything.

"I don't love you," he says while he stares into my eyes. "I don't love you and I'm going back to New York. I want to be left alone. You'll be happy with Matt."

I don't say anything. I can't. I was wrong. Again. I should've listened to Aunt Erma and I should've remembered that I can't trust myself.

"I'm sorry I misunderstood," I say. "You're right. You aren't who I thought you were."

He nods, and then, "Bye, Chloe."

"Goodbye," I whisper.

I reach out and take his hand. I memorize the crinkles at the corners of his eyes and the callouses on his fingertips. "Be happy. Be happy, Nick." That's my greatest desire for him.

"Send me a wedding invite," he says.

I shake my head. "I'm not letting you within a hundred yards of the church. God knows, if you show, the wedding will fall through. Except this time, there'll be no cake." I try to smile, but this time, it's really not funny.

I want to tell him I'll miss him, but I can't. There's so many things I can't say. Finally, after a long silence, Nick pulls his hand from mine.

He leaves. And this time I don't run after him.

29

Nick

I STOP IN VEGAS FOR SHELLY. SHE'S AT AN IMPOUND LOT, BURNED, busted up, undrivable and unfixable. Shelly's dead. I rest my hand on her hood.

"Hey girl. Sorry I let you down."

I run my hand over her blackened metal. Pieces of her frame are melted. Her windows are shattered. Her front bumper is gone and half of her body is caved in and twisted. She'll never be able to drive again. She's a blackened shell. I look at the charred and torn backseat. *The* backseat. I remember the night Chloe and I finally made love. We were so young, but it felt like I'd waited forever for her. That night, I was on top of the world. I believed that things could only get better. It's funny that less than twelve hours later that belief was shattered. I turn away from the backseat, there's nothing left of her. She's gone.

I head back toward the impound office. If I leave Shelly

here they'll crush her for scrap. They'll tear her apart and stamp her into a ball of metal. There'd be nothing left of her at all. I pay the money to break her out of the car graveyard, then I hire a truck to haul her home. The entire trip back feels like a funeral procession.

Back in Romeo, everything returns to the way it was before. I eat, I sleep, I'm left alone. I pick up a few infidelity cases and take photos of people proving to everyone that love isn't real. I contemplate getting out of this field, it's too depressing, even for me. Reed is talking about starting a security firm in Romeo and keeps asking me to partner with him.

Beyond that, there's not much to look forward to in life. Not much at all.

I eat, I sleep, I'm left alone.

After a few days back, Erma calls to settle her bill. She invites me to swing by, so I drive over to the retirement home.

When I arrive, I head to Erma's suite. She's in another kimono-style robe. There's a pot of tea and oatmeal raisin cookies on her table.

"Come in, Nick, come in. Tea, coffee? I know you love my oatmeal raisin. Always a rascal."

She sits down and I perch on the edge of a wooden chair.

"Ah...um..." Huh.

"Eat," she says. Her eyes are sharp and it's clearly an order.

I grab a cookie and take a bite. It's dry and I force the scratchy oats down. She pours coffee and I take a grateful swallow.

"Thank you," I say. "Delicious."

Her eyes narrow and I'm reminded of her hawk like gaze and her uncanny ability to pull secrets out of me when I was a kid. I shift in my seat. I finish the cookie and then end the long silence.

"There's no need to settle," I say. "I'm not submitting a bill.

There's no payment needed, no reimbursement, no cabin, no land. We're all set."

I move to stand.

"Sit down," Erma says in a firm voice.

I sit.

"I heard from Chloe," she says.

The dry cookie I just ate kicks around in my stomach. I want to ask if Chloe's coming back to Romeo, what she's doing, how she is. I want to know anything and everything, and also, nothing. Because no news is good news. I take the safe approach and stay quiet.

Erma takes a sip of tea and watches me over the rim of her china cup. After she sets the cup down she studies me with a shrewd gaze.

"You don't want any payment?"

"No."

"Not even the land? Isn't that what you always wanted? A bit of land to yourself?"

I get the feeling she's watching me like a hawk watches a mouse right before it swoops down and grabs it.

I shift in my seat. "Miss Erma, with all due respect, I'm not taking any payment. The job's done. We're all set."

She picks up the tea pot, it's in a purple cozy, and pours more steaming tea into her cup. Then she adds milk and sugar and stirs it all with a tiny silver teaspoon. She takes a sip and sets the china down.

"Chloe's doing well," she says. "This Matt Smith seems like a perfect gentleman."

This time, I'm ready to hear Chloe's name, and I barely react. I don't think Erma can hear the thundering of my heart.

"I'm glad," I say. My voice comes out hoarse.

"Are you sure you don't want any payment? Anything at all?"

"I'm sure," I say. A drop of sweat falls down the side of my face. I wipe it away. Autumn is here and Erma has her heat cranked high.

"What about a soul mate?" she asks. There's a grandmotherly smile on her face.

"No thank you," I say. Erma's a loose cannon, even if I say no, she may decide to tell me that my soul mate is Brandy, the bully who gave me a wedgie on the first day of kindergarten.

"Ah, I see. You helped Chloe find hers, but you don't want your own."

I look down at my hands. "That's right." My heart gives a hard, jarring thump in my chest.

Erma stands, so I stand too. She sends a brisk smile my way and ushers me to the door.

"You call me when you change your mind," she says.

She holds open the door. That's all? I'm let off this easy? There's a tight heaviness in my chest that's telling me this can't be it.

"We're all set?" I ask.

Erma looks up at me and cocks her head like the hawk I imagined earlier. Then, she swoops in for the kill. "Of course, dear boy," she says, "you did your job. I'm expecting wedding bells this week."

The room tilts and I grab the door handle. I stumble out of Erma's suite. The scent of the retirement home—bleach, air freshener, and cafeteria lunch—hits me and I think I'll be sick. I rush toward the exit and throw open the door. I'm blinded by the harsh sunlight, so I stop and pull in hard breaths of cold air. A crow caws in the tree above me. It sounds like the discordant ringing of wedding bells.

30

Chloe

I LEAN OVER THE EDGE OF MATT'S THIRD-STORY DECK AND WATCH the ocean crash over the shore. It's been three days since Nick left, and every one of them I've spent at Matt's house party. I spend my nights at the hotel, but the days...those are spent talking about art, lounging by the pool, and taking walks on the beach.

When the party started, Matt introduced me to all his friends as the woman he was going to marry. He said it in a joking way, but I could tell there was serious intent underneath. He would look at me each time that he said it and his eyes would lift as he smiled. I always forced myself to smile back.

All the single women at his party looked at me with envy. No one had been able to catch Matt's eye, and here I was, after only a few days, *the woman he wanted to wed.*

I lean farther over the glass railing. It's a long way down and my stomach rolls as I imagine the fall. It would kill me. And isn't that what I've been afraid of? The fall and the crash? Yet, here I am with Matt Smith, my soul mate, and it hurts. Maybe, even more than tumbling down this cliff and falling to the rocks below.

I want Nick. I want him more than I want my "soul mate."

But he doesn't want me. It's funny how life works out. I guess my aunt was right after all. The slider door opens and I turn to see Matt coming out onto the deck. He's wearing what I've come to think of as beach casual, and carrying two glasses of white wine.

"I wondered where you got to," he says.

"Sorry. Is it okay that I explored? I was taking a break from the party." Honestly, everyone's curiosity about me and his constant attention is a lot.

I take the wine glass from him and ask something that's been bothering me for days. "Why do you like me?"

Matt lets out a loud laugh. Sometimes his laugh reminds me of the barking harbor seals that I saw by the beach the other day.

"You say the funniest things," he says.

I frown. "I'm serious."

"So am I. Remember your joke about Cubism? I'm still laughing." He takes another sip and moves closer. "Listen. How can I not like you? You're talented, beautiful, you understand art. We connect."

I make a non-committal sound. "But why?" I ask. I haven't mentioned my Aunt Erma yet and he doesn't know that she predicted we're soul mates. For some reason, I haven't been able to bring it up.

All this interest and solicitousness is all him. He really likes me. A lot. The fact that I argued passionately that it would be like this doesn't elude me. But I guess Nick rubbed off on me more than I realized, because I wonder what his ulterior motives are. What's his angle?

I set the glass down on the flat edge of the railing.

"Why weren't you suspicious of me?" I ask.

He sets his glass down next to mine and tilts his head. His blonde wavy hair falls over his eyebrows. "What do you mean? You're awfully serious." He's still laughing at me.

I scowl and feel like I'm channeling Nick. "I mean, why didn't you question me more? You're a bachelor multi-millionaire and I show up out of nowhere and claim to be a random girl from your childhood. I could be a con-artist. A serial killer. Some sort of insane stalker."

His eyebrows get higher on his forehead and then he barks out a laugh. "But you're not. It's obvious you're not. I mean, look at you." He gestures at my lacy pink dress and my flower-print high heels. His gesture says, *you're so cute and innocent.*

I deepen my scowl and fold my arms over my chest. "But I could be."

"Listen, I'm going to be straight with you."

"Please do."

He takes my hands in his. He has long, tapered artist's fingers. Nothing at all like the rough callouses on Nick's hands.

Matt clears his throat and a blush spreads across his cheeks. "Have you ever had the experience where you make eye contact with someone and there's a zing?"

"Zing?" I say stupidly.

He nods. "I didn't want to say anything, because it all sounds metaphysical and hokey. But when I saw you, I felt like you were the one."

My mouth goes dry and suddenly I feel faint. I blink at the dizziness and try to pull myself together.

"You think I'm crazy," he says. He lets go of my hands. "I knew it was too soon. I knew you'd think I was crazy."

My vision starts to tunnel and there's a roaring in my ears. I lean against the railing.

"Are you okay?" Matt asks.

"I just need a minute."

He stands next to me and looks out over the water. "Is it that other guy? Your friend?"

"No," I say. My head clears and I feel steady again. "No. He doesn't want me."

"Is that what he said?" asks Matt.

"Do you really want to know?"

"Of course. It concerns the woman I'm going to marry." He winks and pushes his blonde hair out of his eyes.

Well..."Yes. He said he doesn't want me."

Matt laughs. "Listen, he was lying. But it's my luck, because I do want you and I'm not afraid to admit it."

"Even if I'm an ax murderer?"

"So cynical," he says.

"What's wrong with you that you trust me so easily?"

"There's nothing wrong with trusting," he says.

"I don't know," I say. But if I trusted, I'd be back in New York right now, knocking down Nick's door, no matter how hard he tried to push me away.

"Can I kiss you?" he asks. He steps closer and looks down at me.

I clench up and have to stop myself from looking away. "O-okay," I say, even though it feels wrong.

He bends down. His lips are cold and dry. I try to relax, but I can't. His hands move to my shoulders and my skin itches under him. He smears his lips across mine and tries to get me to open my mouth, but I'm too stiff. All I can think is that his lips feel like sandpaper and he tastes like raw fish. Finally, he pulls back.

He studies me. "Nothing?" he asks.

I shake my head.

"Well," he says, "it took Michelangelo four years to paint the Sistine Chapel. A masterpiece takes time."

He picks up his wine glass and settles into a comfortable pose looking over the water.

"Speaking of art, what've you been working on?"

I think about my ideas for the new card line. "I've been designing this new series called Dog loves Cat. It's about these two critters that are complete opposites in every way, but eventually they realize they're a perfect match. They complement each other so well that they realize their lives work best when they're together."

He clinks his glass against mine. "That's a spectacular idea. Opposites attract. Listen though, real life doesn't work that way. The best lovers have things in common. But the idea's neat in fiction and art."

"You think?" I ask.

"I do. Will you come by tomorrow? It's the last day my guests are here. I'm sure some of them would like to say goodbye."

I consider it, then, "Okay, yes."

"Good," he says.

I swallow the rest of the white wine. The sweet late harvest Riesling tastes bitter as it goes down. I think being here is one of the stupidest things I've ever done. It feels wrong. While being with Nick, which was wrong, felt unbelievably right.

31

Nick

I'M ON A JOB. IT'S DOWN NEAR THE BORDER OF NEW YORK AND Connecticut. It's a long haul for a job, but it's paying well and is a good distraction. My client told me her "mate" was meeting other males on the side. When confronted, he denied it. Hence, my hiring. I'm at the address she provided at the time she suspected, sitting in my car waiting for someone to show. It's a small upscale boutique shopping mall with expensive restaurants, designer stores and a pet spa. Because it's nearly eleven at night, there are only a few cars in the parking lot.

I sink lower in my seat and lift my camera as a red Maserati pulls in.

"Bingo," I say.

A man gets out of the driver seat. He's wearing sunglasses at night. Of course. He pulls up the collar of his coat, hunches his shoulders, and quickly glances around the parking lot.

"Not suspicious at all," I say. I lift my camera and take a few shots from my car. I zoom in on his face. The guy looks strangely familiar, but I can't place him.

Headlights flood over the parking lot and a Porsche pulls into the spot next to the Maserati. A tall narrow-shouldered man in a red blazer gets out. I snap another photo.

The two men shake hands then step apart. Huh. Not exactly the behavior I've come to expect from cheating spouses. Then, the first guy, the one that looks familiar, goes to the passenger door of his car and pulls out a box.

I zoom in my camera. "Holy..."

That's not a box.

It's a cat carrier. And now I remember where I've seen this guy before. It's Matt Smith Number One. And he's not the one cheating. Cauliflower is.

The two men both carry their cats as they walk toward the luxury pet spa. At first, I'm stunned and my mind goes blank. But then, it's like there's this big neon finger in the sky pointing at Matt Smith.

It's a sign.

The universe is sending me a huge blinking sign that says, *get off your ass and go get your girl.*

All these Matt Smiths, they mean nothing. It was never about them.

It never mattered if it was Matt Smith Number One, Two, or Seventeen. Chloe is mine. My mind races back through all the conversations we had and I remember one in particular.

I'd asked her what a guy could do to prove beyond a doubt that he's the one. A grand gesture, she'd said, a Bollywood-style song and dance with a grand declaration of love. I'd scoffed and said that no man would ever be idiotic or stupid enough to embarrass himself like that.

I watch as Matt Smith walks away. He's my sign.

I'll be that stupid. I'll be that idiotic.

I may not be Chloe's predicted soul mate, but I can still be *the one*.

I jump out of the car and run toward Matt Smith. "Matt. Cauliflower."

Both men turn with shocked and guilty expressions. Then Matt sees my face. "You."

I hold up my hands. "I'm a private investigator. I've been hired to record your breach of mating contract."

"Ridiculous," he says.

The man in the red blazer looks between us and then hightails it back to his Porsche.

Matt Smith sneers. "That male was from a champion line longer than your—"

"Right," I say. "I'm going to report my findings to my client."

"How much can I pay you for your silence?"

"Nothing."

Number One hisses and I hear a long yowl from the cat carrier.

"However, I can give you a few hours before I send my report if you want to admit your affair before I confirm it."

"Why would you do that?" he asks.

I place my future before the fates and roll the dice. "Remember the woman I was with?"

"The one looking for her soul mate?"

I nod. "I want to marry her."

Matt Smith lets out a long, wheezing laugh. "And?" he says when he's finished laughing.

"And she's in California with Matt Smith."

"She found him?" he asks.

"She did."

"So, why would you take her from that?"

I pause, then, "Because I love her."

"If you loved her, you'd let her go," he says.

I shake my head, no.

"I thought that at first, then I realized it was bull. She said she chose me and I didn't believe her. Now she might be marrying Matt Smith and I need to get there to tell her how I feel."

Matt throws back his head and laughs. "You're going to do a grand gesture."

"How do you know about the grand gesture?"

He points at Cauliflower. "I'm an expert in cat mating. They have grand gestures, too."

"Don't want to know," I say.

He shrugs. "You need a private jet," he guesses.

"I need a plane," I agree. "And I need to stop off at a few places on the way to California."

He looks down at Cauliflower. She lets out a happy meow that I recognize as the precursor to a hairball.

"Give me another reason why I shouldn't send you to jail for attempted theft and blackmail?"

I send another prayer up to the fates. "Because your cat really likes me? And deep down you're a romantic?" Where has my cynicism gone? Chloe's worn off on me.

Number One bends down to the door of the carrier and converses with Cauliflower. After a few whispered words and one meow he stands up.

Apparently, my future hangs in the claws of a cat.

I hold my breath.

Matt Smith Number One smirks. "We'll do it," he says.

"Thank you," I say. I'm about to get on a plane, the one thing I said I'd never do, because yes, I'm terrified of flying. But I'm more terrified of losing the woman I love.

I share my plan with Matt and lay out all the cities we need to stop in on the way to L.A.

32

Chloe

IT'S THE MOST BEAUTIFUL SUNSET I'VE EVER SEEN. THE SUN kisses the ocean and spills orange and gold across cerulean waves. The sand reflects like yellow diamonds in the light. Matt and I walk along the beach and I listen to the waves and the birds calling their evening song.

"I'm glad you came today," says Matt. He has on linen pants and a white button-up shirt. His feet are bare. He seems happy, but a little on edge.

"Me too," I say.

I spent the day sitting on the beach under an umbrella finalizing the designs for the Dog loves Cat line. The cat took on a haughty scowl similar to Nick's. I spent an hour imagining the exact shade of Cat's eyes, and when I got it just right, I realized it's the shade that lines Nick's irises. After that, I looked through all my sketches. It was impossible to deny that I'd been drawing scenes of Nick and me. I was illustrating our love story.

I've believed in soul mates my whole life. I also believed that when I found him I'd know without a doubt that he was mine. I haven't trusted myself though, not for a long time. And without trusting myself, I've been blind.

I glance across the beach as the sun dips lower. There are quite a few people out. There's a couple enjoying wine on a blanket. A young mom and dad building a sand castle with their two kids. Two boys throwing a ball in the water. I spot a bigger group of about a dozen men farther down the beach. It looks like they're setting up a party. They have tiki torches, colorful flags and streamers, and music speakers.

"Chloe," Matt says.

"Yes?" I ask. There's something odd about the group up ahead. I have that feeling you get when you know you're being watched. I can feel their attention on me.

"Chloe. I know we've only known each other for a few days," Matt says. "But I feel so connected to you."

I pick up my pace. We're only about twenty feet from the group now. I don't recognize any of them, but they're all looking at me. Then, music starts to play from the sound system behind them. The men start to snap their fingers in time to the song and move in a choreographed dance. Six of the men move to one side and six to another, until they've formed a tunnel. A man walks through the tunnel. One I recognize.

Matt Smith Number One?

But why?

I watch in shock as he slides through the tunnel and spins in a circle. He holds up his cat Cauliflower and waves her paws in the air. What in the world?

Next, Matt Smith the proctologist walks through the tunnel. He's got rubber gloves on and is doing jazz hands.

"Chloe," says the Real Matt.

I turn back to him and he drops down on one knee.

"What?" I shake my head. I glance back at the dancing Matts and the music. Shocker of all shocks, Matt Smith from Colorado stomps across the beach. He doesn't dance, he just twirls what I hope is a fake ax.

"Did you do this?" I ask the real Matt.

But that doesn't make any sense. He doesn't know any of these other Matts.

He doesn't hear me. He's intent on pulling a red velvet box from his pocket. Oh my gosh. He opens it. There's a humungous pink diamond that sparkles in the rays of the setting sun.

"Chloe Daniels...will you be my Sistine Chapel? Marry me."

I stare at him in shock. Then I turn again. A coyote, Matt Number Five, is howling as he dances. How? Then, across the beach, I hear a loud engine roar. A monster truck skids to a stop in the sand.

I know that monster truck. I know the driver. And I know the guy standing in the truck bed dressed like he's in some crazy Bollywood movie.

"Oh, wow," I say.

It's Nick. He's here. He's here for me and he's going to give me a grand gesture.

My whole body floods with warmth and knowing. I see him and I *recognize* him. My soul recognizes him and I don't let fear or mistrust of myself stop that knowledge.

He's mine.

And I'm his.

I start to walk toward him.

"Chloe," calls the Real Matt Smith, "kind of proposing here."

I turn around, "I'm so sorry," I say. "I'm sorry. I can't marry you."

"But…" He looks so confused. "I'm rich. I'm good looking. I'm an artist."

I pull him back to his feet. "Trust me, we're not meant to be. But it was really nice to see you again."

I turn back to Nick and start to run.

"Where are you going?" Matt calls.

"Home," I yell over my shoulder.

But when I turn back to the monster truck, Nick is gone.

33

Nick

CHLOE'S GETTING PROPOSED TO BY NUMBER SEVEN. RIGHT NOW he's on his knees and Chloe's laughing and pulling him up. Dang it.

It's over. I tried and I failed.

I hop down from the truck and lean my head against the metal. Then, I hear her. She's calling me. I lift up my head and come around the truck. Chloe's running toward me. I've never seen anything so beautiful in my life. I take off across the sand toward her. When she reaches me, I grab her and spin her in the air. She laughs as her dress fans out around her and sand flies around us.

Matt Smith Number Two's band is singing an original number, and all the other Matts are singing along. They're doing a terrible job. But it doesn't matter, because Chloe's in my arms.

"What are you doing?" she asks. Her arms are around my shoulders and her legs are wrapped around my hips.

"What does it look like?" I ask.

"Making a fool of yourself for a girl?"

"Damn straight I am. Is it working?"

Her eyes light up and I can see the whole world in them. Our future, our happiness, and our love for one another. She smiles, her lips are so close.

"Eh. Maybe a little," she says. She holds up two fingers and makes the "just a smidge" sign.

"I love you," I say. "I'll love you forever and to the end of the earth. I'll love you if you don't marry me, I'll love you if you do. I'll love you if we have children, I'll love you if we don't. I'll love you if we're poor, I'll love you if we're rich. I'll love you today, I'll love you tomorrow. I'll love you whether I was fated to or not. I'll love you, always and forever."

She pulls me close and buries her face in my neck.

"Well?" I ask.

"Yes," she whispers.

She lifts her face and brings her lips to mine.

"Yes?" I ask.

"Yes. I love you always and forever, too."

I can't contain it. I whoop and spin her around and then I take her mouth in mine and kiss her and kiss her and kiss her.

It lasts for an eternity and we don't stop until I realize the song's over and all the Matts are standing around watching.

"She said yes." My heart is bursting.

I grin at the crowd of Matts as they cheer. Then Matt Smith Number One breaks out the champagne.

"What now?" asks Chloe.

And I'm so happy to have her that I don't have an answer. "I don't know," I say. "Let's think about it tomorrow. Right now, I've got a woman I want to love."

"Good plan," she says.

We skip the champagne and the party on the beach and head for a bed.

34

Chloe

EVERY WOMAN ALIVE IS GIVEN ONE MAN WHO IS GUARANTEED TO turn their life into a monument of awesome. My one man is Nick O'Shea. Every time he shows up my life gets shaken upside down and turned back right.

Aunt Erma always promised that someday I'd find my soul mate. The one man made for me. I thought that fate would tell me who that was, but it turns out, my heart knew.

I look into Nick's eyes as he slides the gold wedding band on my left hand. All three hundred guests let out a riotous cheer. Now, before you go thinking that I'm the most popular girl in town, I have to tell you, half the town just crashed the party.

Aunt Erma's been pretty quiet about how things turned out, saying neither nay nor yay to my decision. I slide the wedding ring onto Nick's hand. It feels like I've come home.

"I now pronounce you man and wife," says Father Green. "You may kiss the bride."

Nick pulls me in and gives me a toe-curling kiss that lasts way longer than most wedding kisses. Everyone goes wild.

When Nick pulls away there's a spark in his eyes. He turns to the crowd and says, "Who wants some cake?"

"Unbelievable," I say.

He laughs, hoists me up and carries me down the aisle. You'd think that nothing could stop him from leaving the church and getting to the street where the limo's supposed to take us to our reception. But when we get to the sidewalk, he stutters to a stop.

"What?" He looks at me in shock. "How?"

I give a secret smile. "Maybe, since I'm mega rich from all the Dog loves Cat sales, I got her fixed up as your wedding gift."

He doesn't say anything. He just stands there and stares at Shelly. She's all gleaming and beautiful and looking brand spanking new. Let me tell you, it wasn't easy getting her fixed.

"Is it okay?" I ask. I'm nervous now that he's seen her and hasn't said anything for nearly a minute. "Nick?"

"Sparky," he says. When he looks down at me, his eyes are filled with a heat I recognize. Thank goodness.

"The backseats are gen-u-ine leather," I say. "Very comfortable."

He grins and hurries toward the car. He pops me in the front seat and folds the train of my wedding dress in my lap. He runs around to the driver side. When Shelly roars to life he turns to me and smiles.

"Did I mention lately that I love you?" he asks.

With the engine purring and wedding rings on our fingers, I don't think I could be any happier.

"You may have," I say.

"We're going to be late to our reception," he says.

"You better believe it."

He pulls Shelly onto the road and I reach out to take his hand. When I look in her backseat, I notice a present.

"What's that?" I ask. I reach for the gift. It's wrapped in red paper and a gold bow. On the card it says, *Open Immediately*.

I carefully untie the bow and pull open the wrapping paper. I stare at the gift in shock.

"Do you see this?" I ask.

Nick looks. Then he looks again. Then he pulls over.

We both stare at the photograph.

"That's me," I say.

I'm two years old. I'm wearing a pink frilly bathing suit and I'm sitting in a kiddie pool in my backyard.

"And that's me," says Nick.

He's got black hair, chubby cheeks, and he's sitting in the pool with me.

"And we're kissing," I say.

I run my hands over the photograph. Nick and I are two years old and we're kissing in a kiddie pool in my backyard.

"Unbelievable," he says.

"You're my soul mate," I say.

"Yeah, Sparky. I already knew that."

Then I start to laugh. Unbelievable. I roll down the window and I chuck the photograph into the woods. "Yeah. So did I. So did I."

I lean over and give Nick the second of many, many more kisses as husband and wife.

Then we pull back onto the road and start the first day of the rest of our lives.

THE END

GET A BONUS EPILOGUE FOR CHLOE AND NICK

Want more Chloe and Nick? Read what happens after the wedding - an exclusive bonus epilogue for newsletter subscribers only.

When you join the Sarah Ready Newsletter you get access to sneak peaks, insider updates, exclusive bonus scenes and more.

Join Today!

www.sarahready.com/newsletter

ALSO BY SARAH READY

Stand Alone Romances:

Hero Ever After

The Fall in Love Checklist

Soul mates in Romeo Series:

Chasing Romeo

Love Not at First Sight

Find more books by Sarah Ready at:

www.sarahready.com/romance-books

ABOUT THE AUTHOR

Sarah Ready is the author of *The Fall in Love Checklist* and *Hero Ever After*. She writes contemporary romance and romantic comedy. *Chasing Romeo* is the first book in her new Soul Mates in Romeo romance series. You can find her online at www.sarahready.com.

Stay up to date, get exclusive epilogues and bonus content. Join Sarah's newsletter at www.sarahready.com/newsletter.

Made in the USA
Monee, IL
25 June 2023

37397077R00129